MW00696428

Virginia Ghosts

Virginia Ghosts

Copyright © 2005 by Sweetwater Press

Produced by Cliff Road Books

All rights reserved. No part of this book may be reproduced in any form or by any electronic or mechanical means, including information storage and retrieval systems, without written permission from the publisher.

ISBN: 1-58173-509-X

Book design by Pat Covert

Printed in the United States of America

Virginia
Ghosts

they are among us

Ian Alan

SWEET WATER PRESS

Table of Contents

They Are Among Us

They Are Among Us

My name is Ian Alan. Among other things, I collect ghosts. My fascination with ghosts, phantoms, and other unbidden guests began as a small child in Louisiana. This is a place known for strange and mysterious happenings. Nearly everyone had a family story that revolved around the supernatural.

Our household was no different, for we had two ghosts who subtly affected our lives. One was an elderly woman who had died in the house long before we moved in. We regarded her with great respect. She often warned us of small calamities and childhood dangers that were about to happen. Occasionally, in more mischievous moments, she would rearrange the canned goods and pots in my mother's kitchen. As annoying as that could be, everyone in our family regarded her as a protective and benevolent spirit. Our other guest was quite the opposite.

I was the only member of my family who could see the man clad in dark clothes that hung on him like a heavy winter coat. Still, we could sense his presence, and it made us all uncomfortable. It became clear very early on that the old woman was there to protect us from the dark man as they battled in the shadows for stewardship over the family. It was in this environment that I learned to see, speak to, and interact with ghosts.

In ensuing years I traveled all over the globe tracking and "catching" phantoms, employing techniques that could isolate, make visible, and even banish malevolent spirits. More often, I was merely a witness to the spirits and their timeless activities. The spirit world is a viable dimension that intersects with our own. The activity of ghosts can tell us just as much about ourselves as living beings as it can about what occurs after we are no longer living.

No place on earth is this more true than in the southern United States. Spectral tales dramatically underscore every facet of life in the American South. From the founding through the Civil War to modern times, ghosts and spirits have been a vital part of our Southern culture. For more than two hundred years, they have shaped and influenced us, and I have often wondered if we would be truly comfortable knowing the extent of their influence. Surely that is a question that each of us must answer on our own.

As you read the stories and true accounts that follow, ask yourself if there have been moments in your life when something other than your Savior has guided or moved you this way or that. Moments of intuition, feelings of dread, warnings that appeared out of nowhere, and more palpable events have traditionally been the language that ghosts employ to communicate with the living. Occasionally, they resort to visitation as a way to get our attention.

Have you seen someone who is out of place or recollected a conversation that you can't remember having with anyone living? Well, many people have experienced these things, and much, much more. Read on and ask yourself, "Could this ever happen to me?" I can tell you from experience that if you live or travel in the South, sooner or later, you will meet at least one of our ghosts. Sometimes it will be a kind spirit while other times, well ... not so kind. What will you take away from the experience—that is, if you are allowed to leave?

Ian Alan

The Ghostly Guardian

The Ghostly Guardian

The ghost of Thomas Jefferson Beale walks among us. Now, his spirit isn't confined to some ancestral home or some family cemetery, or even a national cemetery. His spirit is confined in three handwritten letters, all written in cipher.

Somewhere between Roanoke and Lynchburg in Bedford County, Virginia, is probably the most famous and notably the largest buried treasure in American history. Thomas Jefferson Beale, along with thirty companions, had made a fortune somewhere in the western United States. Upon returning to his native Virginia, he buried his share of the fortune in a secret underground vault. The whereabouts of this large vault are detailed in three letters that are written entirely in short strings of numbers. Thomas Jefferson Beale buried this treasure in 1821. For generations since, code breakers and cryptologists have been trying to solve the puzzle. They have been unsuccessful to this very day.

The treasure itself is composed of some three tons of gold and gems that, some say, were obtained by the fortune hunters under dubious circumstances. The letters containing the clues to its precise location surfaced about three years after Beale's mysterious disappearance. There are even those who say that Beale was buried with his treasure and protects it still.

Early attempts to decipher the letters were near impossible until it was discovered that Beale had a penchant for the events surrounding our nation's founding. Based solely on the fact that his first and middle names were Thomas Jefferson, an inheritor of the encoded letters discovered that the Declaration of Independence was a key to breaking the code in one of the letters. In the first letter, using the Declaration of Independence as a numeric word key, an amateur cryptologist was able to decipher the instructions that, at some distance south of Buford, a town in Bedford County, was a stone crypt of specified dimensions buried six feet underneath the ground.

The crypt contained three tons of gold, silver, and gems stored in large iron pots. Apparently, the message revealed that the men had acquired the precious metal in the western part of the United States, and the gems from another venture. Details were vague as to whether the treasure had been gained legally or not. Likewise, it has always been unclear as to what the other members of Beale's party had done with their share. Possibly, there had been some additional shenanigans that allowed Beale to obtain it. No one knows for sure.

In any event, it appears that Thomas Jefferson Beale had the lion's share of the gains, and he wanted to bury it so no one could find it. Prior to embarking on a long journey, Beale sealed the three letters in a strongbox and entrusted it to a close friend. Beale requested that the box remain sealed for ten years and only opened if he did not return. He promised the friend that he would send the appropriate word keys necessary to decipher the coded messages. Unfortunately, the friend never received them.

The actual three letters themselves have been favorite subjects for both amateur and professional cryptanalysts for many years. In 1972, there was a symposium given by the Univac Corporation called "The Beale's Cipher Symposium," where they employed the world's most advanced computers of the time to try and break the cipher. Even though the most experienced code breakers across the country got together to work on the Beale Cipher, they had no luck; they weren't able to break the cipher at all. To this day, it remains unbroken. Neither the Declaration of Independence nor any other of the founding documents could be used to decipher the remaining two letters. So only one letter of the three handwritten letters with the short strings of numbers has ever been deciphered.

Solving puzzles, for some, can start off as a hobby

and turn into either a career or an obsession; sometimes it can become both. That's how it was for mathematics professor and code breaker, Winn Husnian.

Winn couldn't remember a time in his life when he wasn't fond of reciting prayers and hymns or nonsense rhymes and poems. In fact, he had always used recitation to calm his mind and organize his thoughts. During the night as a child, he would sing to drive away the monsters that lived in his closet and underneath his bed. He used the recitation of the Hamlet soliloquy as a way to cope with the difficult times of a teenager. As a college student majoring in mathematics, Winn created even more ingenious methods of recitation to quiet his mind and focus his mental powers. Eventually, his methods became a sophisticated coping strategy to deal with the stresses of college life. Little did he know that his skills at recitation and mathematics would lead him to the most intriguing puzzle he would ever encounter.

One night Winn Husnian found himself in the role of amateur cryptanalyst, attempting, yet again, to crack the Beale cipher. It was destined to be a very eventful evening.

It had been hours since he began staring at disparate groups of Beale numbers, trying to find some sort of new clue to the code. Finally, in an attempt to focus his thinking process, he began reciting the numbers aloud, one after the other, one after the other.

"If I could just view it a different way," he thought, "if I can touch it a different way, then I might be able to figure out what the numeric sequence is."

Even as he continued to recite aloud the answer eluded him. Was it a Rail Fence Code? Was it a typical cipher disguised to look like a complicated one? Was it a transposition or an alphanumeric combination? Winn wasn't sure, and it was beginning to frustrate him.

"If I keep repeating it over and over and over and over in my mind," he thought, "then I might be able to see something new that will give me a clue to what kind of cipher it is." It wasn't long before he was reciting the string of numbers as if it were some type of mystical spell. The more he recited the numbers aloud, the stranger things got in the room where he was sitting. Subtle forces were at work.

Winn heard himself reciting the numbers, and it sounded very strange to him. "4, 7, space," he proclaimed loudly. He continued, "9, 10, 12, space, 12, 11, space, 10, space, 7, 7, 1." Over and over again, he would recite the numbers. When read silently, the numbers were bland and lifeless. When read aloud, however, they took on a living quality. Eventually, as he listened to himself entranced in the cadence of reciting the numbers aloud, his spoken words began to hum and pulsate with an eerie power, reverberating off the walls of his office. The walls creaked and the lights dimmed and flickered. He paused briefly and looked around. He was alone, so he continued reciting the numbers over and over again, as if he was chanting or reading from a hymnal.

"I am just reciting numbers," he thought. But as he repeated the strings of numbers over and over again, the dimensions of his office began to change. The walls appeared closer at first and, then, farther back. Colors began to shift, change, and spin throughout the room. Winn thought that he might be passing out. It was all he could do to keep reciting the numbers aloud.

Suddenly, Winn felt a space opening up in his chest and then closing again. He felt his breath shortening and experienced a tingling on the back of his neck and the top of his head. He opened and closed his hands clenching his fingers nervously as he recited the next group of numbers—"7, 12, space, 11, 7, 8, space, 8, space, 7, 2, 3"—over and over again.

"7, 3," he said, frantically opening and closing his fists. Winn would inhale and hold his breath and wait.

"What am I waiting for?" he thought, "What's the next number I should say?" Then he remembered the next string of numbers. Then he would say them aloud, declaiming them to the walls around him: "8, space, 2, 9, 9, space, 2, 1, 7, space, 3." The walls seemed to alternately open up and close in around him. Then the air started to become thick. Winn was having trouble breathing. His palms were sweating. He kept reciting the numbers over and over again.

Winn Husnian was becoming exhausted by the ordeal. He wondered if he should continue or throw in the towel. He had just decided to quit when the air became thick as honey and cloyed in his throat. Winn could barely breathe and began fighting for air. He was silent now, but the numbers had done their work. Winn looked up to see a shimmering shape form in front of him. It was the shape of a man—the shape of an angry man. The visage became more defined and distinct. It was trying to say something to him, but Winn couldn't make it out. Was the ghostly shape trying to convince him of something? "Who is this man?" he thought. The mathematician had the answer as soon as he asked himself the question.

From every historical description he had read, the shape standing before him was Thomas Jefferson Beale. The ghostly vision gestured toward him in an animated fashion as if trying to communicate through his movements alone. Entreating, reaching out with outstretched hands, the ghost was trying to say something to Winn. Whatever the message, Beale's gestures conveyed a sense of urgency.

"Is he telling me to stop what I'm doing?" Winn thought. "Is he trying to silence me and keep me from saying the numbers aloud?"

As he gasped for air, it occurred to Winn that the numbers must be some sort of spell. Perhaps it was the arrangement of the groups or merely his vocalization of them that set the mystic wheels turning.

He decided to address the ghost that stood before him. Winn gathered his strength against the tightening in his chest and said, "Thomas Jefferson Beale, where is your treasure vault? Give me the clues to the whereabouts of your three tons of gold and gems." There was no response from the wraith, so he asked again. This time he was more demanding in his tone. "Thomas Jefferson Beale, it is time that you told me precisely where your treasure is." It looked as if the ghost was about to answer—or was something else about to happen, something that Winn Husnian wasn't prepared for?

The silent ghost of Thomas Jefferson Beale lunged at the mathematician and struck at him with massive hands. The first blow struck Winn on the side of his head, while the other punched him squarely in the chest. Winn reeled backwards and collapsed on the floor. The ghost reached down, grabbed the choking man under each arm, and lifted him to his feet. Winn was staring directly into the face of a dead man whose menacing glare pushed even the fear of suffocation from his mind.

"I have to save myself!" he thought. Not knowing what else to do, Winn tried to recite. Before he could utter a sound, Beale's ghost pulled him closer and, in a harsh whisper, spat the words, "No more!"

Those two words echoed through Winn's head as the ghost released him and allowed the would-be code breaker to collapse on the floor in a heap. A great blackness seemed to rise up from the floor, and Winn Husnian lost consciousness.

Winn regained consciousness in an ambulance. In the emergency room, a doctor asked him how long had it been since he had an asthma attack this severe. Winn tried to explain to the ER staff that he wasn't an asthmatic, but no matter how hard he tried, the doctors would have none of it. "No one has an asthma attack as bad as this one without a significant history," they said.

Winn spent the next two days in a hospital bed. He had plenty of time to reflect on the events surrounding the Beale Cipher. He wondered what would've happened if he had managed to keep reciting the numbers aloud. Would he have finally discovered the secret of the code, or would Thomas Jefferson Beale tell him that he didn't want anyone to find his hidden treasure vault? Winn Husnian decided that he might not survive the latter and resolved to heed the ghost's injunction, "No more."

Professional cryptologists and historians have

determined several things about the Beale Cipher. Namely, that it is a real message and is, indeed, a code. There have been other cryptanalysts and other groups that have tried to decipher the Beale letters, but none have been able to make any headway. No clues. No key. Yet, only one person spoke the mathematical incantation aloud, and these days, at least, he spends his time in other pursuits. Content to let someone else solve the puzzle, Winn Husnian put the Beale Cipher behind him.

It remains unsolved to this day.

Ezra, the Cemetery Cat

Ezra, the Cemetery Cat

Ezra the cat moves through the tombstones and monuments of Bruton Parish cemetery largely unnoticed by the residents of Williamsburg. This isn't because cats are quiet and stealthy by nature. No, Ezra goes unnoticed because Ezra is a ghost cat.

Ezra hasn't always frequented the cemetery and the quaint restored town of Old Williamsburg. He used to wander the streets and alleyways like any other self-respecting feline. When he was a living corporeal animal, Ezra had a master by the name of Isaac Martin. Isaac had spent his whole life living in Williamsburg, though all of his people came from Roanoke, Virginia. By trade, he was a shoe repairman and made quite a decent living at it. He was schooled in the old style of the cobblers and was blessed with an eye for flattery, especially when it came to selling shoes to the ladies.

Isaac Martin also had the skill of being at the right place at the right time. He had never finished school, but was a brilliant child. He was already a voracious reader while the other children were out in the yard playing. On his seventeenth birthday, Isaac was walking down a Williamsburg street pondering the notion of learning a trade so he could support himself. At that very moment, he quite literally bumped into an old cobbler who was looking for a young apprentice. They struck up a conversation, and Isaac began working for the old cobbler the very next day.

It was during this apprenticeship that Isaac and Ezra met. Ezra had been your typical street kitty and needed a home. Isaac, being at heart a good-natured young man, immediately took him in. From the first moment they were together, the two were inseparable. At the end of the day, Ezra would walk with Isaac back to the house where he lived, and the next morning the two would walk back to the shoe repair store. During business hours, customers would come in, and Ezra would greet them with a purr and a wink while Isaac tended to their repairs.

After only a couple of years of apprenticeship, the old cobbler died, and Isaac Martin inherited the business. It was just Isaac and Ezra tending to the shoe needs of the people of Old Williamsburg. During the day, they would greet customers and repair shoes, but in the evening, they would spend time with each other while Isaac fed his voracious appetite for books. Isaac Martin was particularly interested in history, genealogy, and those topics that most people would consider rather esoteric and strange.

The Martins were distant relatives of Nathaniel Bacon, a prominent name in Virginia history. Nathaniel, in turn, was related to Sir Francis Bacon. Isaac engaged in continual research of the Martin and the Bacon family histories, both in Virginia and prior to that in England. Isaac would spread his books, papers, and notes across the floor, detailing his self-made compendium of the Bacon family history. Ezra would lie across the paper, letting his tail swish this way and that, and generally amused himself while his master studied, researched, and wrote. There were even times when Isaac found himself unable to locate a specific entry or specific piece of paper—or even a volume somewhere in their small home—and Ezra would invariably find that piece of paper for him. "Thank you, Ezra," Isaac would say frequently. Ezra would just purr, smile, and find another bundle of papers to catnap on.

The history that Isaac Martin was accumulating was fascinating. Of particular interest to him was Bacon's Rebellion of 1676. Most historical works considered this rebellion to be the beginnings of the revolutionary fervor in America. Almost one hundred years later, the small spark had built to a conflagration that resulted in the American Revolution. Isaac, however, had discovered more than just a few pertinent details about Bacon's Rebellion. His analysis of the situation was that Bacon's

Rebellion had nothing to do with revolutionary sentiment. It was, in fact, a power struggle between two shallow and self-centered colonial leaders.

Nathaniel Bacon himself was in his youth a troublemaker and a lay-about. Nathaniel's father had sent him to Virginia in hopes that life in the Colonies would season his son and turn him into a man. Nathaniel, however, had other ideas. His dislike of physical labor—and almost anything that remotely looked like work—was noted by everyone he met. Yet he was very well educated and eloquent, and soon worked his way into old Virginia high society.

Isaac Martin couldn't help but be a little bit envious of this rogue in his family lineage. He would often talk to Ezra regaling the feline with whatever he had discovered about his distant relative. He would tend to embellish a little bit when explaining things to the cat, making his roguish relation a bit more of a daredevil or a conquering hero, sometimes painting him as a dangerous adventurer. But the part of the story of Nathaniel Bacon that fascinated Isaac Martin the most was the legend that he had secreted somewhere in Williamsburg a cache of papers, documents, plans, books, gold, and jewels to be opened up at a later date by some member of his family.

Among the more interesting things that were supposed to be in this cache was proof that Sir Francis

Bacon was the firstborn son of England's Queen Elizabeth. Supposedly, there were documents that detailed the intrigues by which powerful members in the English court sought to keep Sir Francis Bacon away from the throne. There were also detailed notes by Bacon on these various members of the English court that could be used against them to wrest power from their hands. Other items rumored to be in this bundle of documents were several letters that provided conclusive proof that Sir Francis Bacon wrote all of the literary works attributed to William Shakespeare.

Over the years, the more Isaac researched, the stranger the information about this cache of papers became. The secret documents and many more like them were supposedly contained in a ten-foot-by-ten-foot secret vault that was buried sixteen feet below the Bruton Parish Episcopal Church cemetery. Using a complex series of codes and anagrams inscribed on various national monuments, headstones, and gravestones throughout the area, Nathaniel left detailed instructions about how to find the vault. As he was deciphering these clues, Isaac also found information about Francis Bacon's plan to establish a world government based on the mystical teachings of Rosicrucianism.

The vault was, in fact, a secret Rosicrucian tomb constructed to exacting mystical specifications. Other vaults of this kind are located in England and throughout Europe. Isaac decoded information explaining that the American Revolution had been planned at the time of Nathaniel Bacon by the Rosicrucian brotherhood. They had also plotted the French Revolution. That particular experiment didn't work out as well as the brotherhood had planned. The introduction of democracy was supposed to be the death-knell of the Old World monarchies—the same political power structure that had robbed Sir Francis Bacon of his rightful inheritance to the throne of England.

One night, Isaac was staring at the papers, notes, and books spread out on the floor of his small house when all of a sudden he broke the final piece of the code. At that moment, he was aware that the secret Rosicrucian vault was located ten feet west of a gravesite bearing the name of Anne. The final calculations told him that the secret vault was between ninety and one hundred ten feet northwest of the front door of the parish church. "Eureka!" Isaac said playfully. "I found it!" And he began to look around for Ezra to tell him the great news. But Ezra was nowhere to be found. "Here, Ezra. Here, kitty," Isaac said, but still no Ezra. Isaac didn't give it too much thought as he turned back to his books and notes to recheck his calculation. So several hours had passed before he realized Ezra hadn't shown up for dinner yet, and he became worried.

29

Then, at about midnight, he heard a mournful cry, and he went out to find Ezra in a very bad state. Ezra had obviously been the victim of a neighbor dog. He was covered with blood and limping, with one eye badly wounded. Isaac took him back to the house and cleaned him up. Over the next few days, he nursed Ezra back to health.

Ezra wasn't quite the same after that. He had a permanent limp. His tail was bent and crooked, and he was blind in one eye. It was clear that the dog attack had taken a great toll on the cat. Still, he loved greeting people in Isaac Martin's shoe shop, and everybody was very sympathetic. He got more than one free fish or meal of table scraps given to him in sympathy by the shop-goers.

Several months went by, and it became clear that Ezra wasn't long for this world. His injuries had just been too much for him. He didn't walk back to the house from the shop any more. Isaac put him in a little side bag and talked to him as he walked down the street. Then one Friday evening, as Isaac was regaling Ezra with tales of Nathaniel Bacon and the hidden Rosicrucian vault in the Williamsburg cemetery, Ezra quietly slipped off this mortal coil.

Although Ezra's death hadn't been unexpected, Isaac was distraught. His friend, his confidante, was no more, and he wondered what he was going to do next. Then Isaac had an interesting notion. He sneaked onto the grounds of the Episcopal Church cemetery and very quietly buried Ezra in the cemetery. He was careful to arrange the grave so that no one would be the wiser. "Well, Ezra, old friend," Isaac said, "we've talked a lot about this cemetery and this area and this church. It seems only fitting that this should be your final resting place." He said a quiet prayer, and with that, bid his friend farewell and went home.

It was several weeks later that Isaac first noticed a flash of familiar movement out of the corner of his eye when he passed the church cemetery. He stopped and he looked, but he couldn't see anything, so he went on to work. Later that evening as he was coming home, he again saw something moving amongst the headstones and graves. Then, as he got farther away from the cemetery, he began to feel that someone was unmistakably following him. So he turned and he looked. Off in the distance, he saw the outline of a cat. But this was no ordinary cat. There was the same limp and the same bent tail of Ezra. As soon as Isaac said his name, the ghost cat straightened up and started to walk toward him—and then vanished altogether. Isaac decided that his eyes were just playing tricks on him, and he needed some rest. Perhaps he would dispense with the research and reading this evening; his heart really hadn't been in it since Ezra had died, and most of his research and leads had gone unattended. Isaac missed Ezra very much.

Still, the story of a mysterious Rosicrucian vault buried somewhere near where he walked every day held its fascination over him. So when he got home, he spread his notes and his papers and his latest stack of reading on the floor and went to go make himself a cup of tea. When he came back in, out of the corner of his eye, he was able to glimpse Ezra, sitting on top of a pile of his research papers. But this time, he didn't call his name. He remembered what had happened last time. When he addressed the spectral feline by name, Ezra vanished. So he just continued to be about his business while keeping watch on the ghostly shape out of the corner of his eye.

Isaac wasn't sure how you were supposed to treat a ghost, much less a ghost cat. Still, though, Ezra and he had been great friends, and this had been Ezra's home for many years. So Isaac Martin just decided to act like everything was perfectly normal. Over the next few months, whenever Isaac caught sight of Ezra's ghost, he would address it as if the cat were still living, asking him how his day was, talking to him about people who had come into the shop, and regaling him with more details and information about his family tree. It wasn't very long before Isaac was treating Ezra as if he were still living and breathing there in his house. Ezra seemed to like that just fine.

One night, as Isaac and Ezra the ghost were going over notes, papers, and reading material, Ezra began nosing one particular book. Isaac picked up the book and opened it on the floor and began to slowly turn pages while Ezra's ghost just circled the perimeter of the room. Then, as Isaac Martin turned one page, Ezra leapt toward the book and put his ghostly paw on one page. On that page was an anagram, and, though Isaac couldn't understand what significance this anagram had, he set to work solving it. He was in for a surprise. In short order, he had before him the final piece of the puzzle; the necessary clue to discerning the specific resting place of Nathaniel Bacon's ten-by-ten-foot secret vault.

"Is this it?" Isaac Martin said. Ezra's ghost just purred. "Well, what do you think, Ezra?" Isaac Martin said. "Do you think we should we go to the graveyard and dig this thing up?" The ghostly cat just purred and headed for the door.

Isaac grabbed a shovel and a small lantern. He would have to be very careful, but he was determined to find some specific evidence as to the existence of the vault buried beneath the ground. His new piece of information, which was revealed in the anagram, actually placed the vault much closer to the surface than his previous research had indicated. But it also alluded to a series of mysterious documents that was supposed to reveal the Rosicrucian mysteries. Isaac had seen enough of these anagrams to know that they were real and worth investigating.

"All right, Ezra," he said to his ghostly companion as they got near the cemetery. "The anagram says we really only need to dig two feet below the surface right about here at this spot to hit the edge of the vault. Once we do that, then we can figure out what to do next."

Looking around carefully to make sure he would go unnoticed, Isaac began to dig. Several dense bushes and two small trees shielded the spot where he began digging. Isaac had to stop only occasionally to stay hidden from the odd passerby. After all, there weren't that many people out after midnight. Ezra's ghost just circled the work site as Isaac continued to explore and test the ground with his shovel. Then Isaac Martin hit pay dirt. One stroke of his shovel fell with a metallic thud that signaled metal striking some sort of stone. He dug carefully but quickly and uncovered what looked to be a piece of marble or granite with inscriptions carved on it in some ancient tongue. It looked like Hebrew, but it was different. Isaac recognized the inscriptions. They were the secret code language of the Rosicrucian mystics.

"This is it, Ezra—we've found it!" Isaac said in a loud whisper. It was then that Isaac Martin reached out and touched the inscribed stone, and when he did, his hand stuck to it as if magnetized. Pain shot through his arm and shoulder and up into his neck and face. He tried to pull away, but he couldn't. His palm was securely fastened to the cold surface of the stone. He wanted to shriek for help, but for some reason couldn't muster the strength. Ezra just sat by the edge of the site and stared at him peacefully. No matter how Isaac struggled, he couldn't free himself.

His mind was awash with images of ancient diagrams and Egyptian symbols—of stacks of paper and glittering jewels and gold. He saw the face of Nathaniel Bacon as well as the face of Sir Francis Bacon, the gentleman who had started it all. Whatever else Nathaniel Bacon had brought over from England and put in the vault, it had to be more than ordinary paper. The onrush of images and feelings convinced Isaac that there was a daring release of energy coming from the vault. But in reality, his very life was being sucked down into the earth. All the while, Ezra purred and swished his tail.

Local storytellers disagree as to precisely what happened next in this mysterious chain of events. Some say Isaac Martin died there in the graveyard in the presence of no one but his ghostly pet. Others say he disappeared, body and soul, deep into the earth or into the small shallow hole he'd dug. Still others say that he survived the encounter only to go insane some years later.

But the only one who really knows the story is Ezra the ghost cat. If you're lucky, you can still see him moving in and around the cemetery near the Episcopal Church. If he could talk, Ezra would probably tell you that true friends are never really separated. Not even in death. He would also tell you that there's something new inside the ten-foot-by-ten-foot vault secretly buried beneath the earth in this part of Old Williamsburg.

There's something more than mystic Rosicrucian documents or undiscovered Shakespearean plays—there's also the ghost of his former master. To this day, when the moon is bright, you can still see Isaac Martin walking among the tombstones and headstones of the cemetery with his beloved cat, Ezra.

The Fairy Stones
of Bull Mountain

The Fairy Stones of Bull Mountain

John Dudley was a moonshiner. In fact, he came from a long line of moonshiners. John's great-grandfather had started the family tradition in the southern Virginia hills near Martinsville. The business had been so very profitable that it ended up being passed down from generation to generation like so much china and silverware. John's father had been known to the local consumers of illegal liquor as "Big John," and big he was. They called his son "Little John," and even though he was smaller than his father in physical stature, Little John Dudley had a big reputation. Nobody could hide a still or make shine better than John.

Even though his father, grandfather, and great-grandfather occasionally experienced brushes with the law, the reigning Dudley moonshiner had never been caught or even bothered by the sheriff. No matter how hard the authorities tried, they could never find John's still—actually, stills. For a while, the revenuers weren't sure that he even existed. Some thought that he was probably just a myth. But the local people were getting their moonshine from someplace, so they kept looking—but to no avail. The revenue men had no idea how he did it. But John Dudley was completely aware of the reason he'd never been caught, or even seen for that matter. John, you see, always wore his fairy stone next to his heart.

Fairy stones are powerful magical charms to the people of southern Virginia. This entire area in the Virginia hills is known for all sorts of weird happenings: ghosts and sounds, floating lights, and strange creatures abound in the folklore of this particular part of the state. Residents there preserve a whole host of mysterious tales, but the legends of the fairy stones are among the most common. Fairy stones have the ability to ward off all kinds of evil. If you find just exactly the right kind of fairy stone around Bull Mountain plateau forty-four miles west of Martinsville, then you will possess a powerful piece of magic.

Geologists refer to fairy stones as cruciform crystals, or naturally-occurring crystal crosses. The cross-shaped crystals are referred to as "penetrating twins" because the crystals grow into each other at angles ranging from sixty to ninety degrees. John's grandfather had often spoken about the lore of these crosses.

He told his grandson that three kinds of fairy stone crosses could be discovered in and around Bull Mountain plateau. There's a simple Roman-style cross, which is supposed to grant the wearer great physical and mental prowess. There was also the Saint Andrew's cross, which looks like a big "X" and is supposed to unify the forces of heaven and hell and grant the wearer the ability to traverse those realms. But the most prized fairy stone cross is the "cross of eight points," or the Maltese cross, which—when worn over the heart—grants the wearer the power of precognitive sight, hearing, and the gift of invisibility. Little John Dudley instantly recognized that the powers granted by the eight-pointed cross would come in handy to a moonshiner, and he was determined to find one.

John was still a young man when he used his bare hands to dig a Maltese cross fairy stone out of the Virginia hills. He formed a makeshift necklace with a length of his own bootlace and hung the cross around his neck. Almost instantly, he felt different. He could see clearer and could hear things that no one else could hear. But mostly, he had the ability to conceal himself. If his intention to go about unnoticed was strong enough while he wore the cross, John Dudley was quite literally invisible. As long as he wore his fairy stone, he'd never be found, and his stills would never be discovered. He always wanted to be the best moonshiner the Dudley family had ever produced. With the cross constantly hanging around his neck, he was able to do just that.

Now, legend has it, once you find a fairy stone and

wear it near your heart, it's very dangerous to take it off. In fact, if it is ever removed, great disaster will follow the wearer. Immense powers are granted anyone who wears a fairy stone, and to take it off is to rudely reject that power. The old timers say that when the forces of the underworld start to work, it's best not to offend them. Even John's grandfather had told gruesome stories about those unfortunate souls that offended the dark powers of the Virginia hills and how they were damned for all eternity. John never dreamed that he might become one of them.

Late one evening, John Dudley returned to his cabin, having completed a full day of dispensing liquor to his local customers and tending his stills. All in all, it had been a typical day for him, save for one event.

One of his best stills located near the Pyramids of Dan, a twin rock formation in the area, had been giving him problems. He had been trying to adjust the still's output by adding more copper tubing when he heard voices and the sounds of people approaching. Assuming they were revenuers, he hid near the two tower-like formations. For what seemed like hours, he eluded the sounds and voices but was unable to catch sight of anyone at all. Though he wondered who was looking for him, John knew that he would never be caught. He was safe as long as he wore the eight-pointed cross.

Now, as he opened the door to his cabin, he mulled over the idea that it might be time to make his talisman more secure. For years, he had worn his fairy stone and never taken it off. But his hastily made necklace was now becoming thin and threadbare, and he knew that if he wasn't careful, he'd be in the woods one day, and the cross would fall off. And that would be the last thing that he wanted. So he decided to take a chance that evening and remove the fairy stone cross to make a new lanyard that was more secure than the old one.

He set to work with a piece of leather and some linen string. When he thought he was ready, he removed the fairy stone cross from his neck and started to attach it to the new lanyard. But as soon as he removed his cross from around his neck, his vision began to shift and his hearing began to change.

Suddenly, he found himself in a room full of ghosts. They were all standing around John Dudley at the table, and they were staring at him with glowing eyes. The ghosts were all in various stages of decay and clarity. But they all seemed to be fixated on what John was doing, staring at the cross that he had just removed from his neck. He heard unearthly words echoing through his head. "Give it to us! Give us the stone!" they demanded.

Quickly, John put the cross back around his neck and held it close to his heart, and the images faded. Not quite knowing what to do next, he slowly removed the cross from around his neck—and the phantoms reappeared. He passed the cross with the old lanyard quickly around his neck, but as he was doing so, the string broke, and the cross fell to the floor, shattering into a dozen pieces. The phantoms were clearly visible now, all milling around John Dudley as he scrambled to the floor to try and collect the pieces. But no matter how hard John tried, his ghostly entourage closed the area around him tighter and tighter. The anger exuded by the specters at the destruction of the stone cross was thick in the air, and they meant to vent their rage on the moonshiner who lay upon the floor. John screamed aloud, and his desperate shriek echoed through the trees.

Local legend has it that, unable to gather and reassemble the pieces of his fairy stone cross, John ran screaming from his cabin in the direction of Bull Mountain plateau. He knew that his very life and sanity depended on his finding another fairy stone and wearing it securely around his neck. Along the way, as he darted through the woods, he caught glimpses of other ghosts who could now see him clearly and began moving in John's direction. The damned souls of previous cross wearers pursued him as if driven by their dark master's whip. Frantically, Little John Dudley ran toward Bull Mountain plateau.

But he was never to make it.

Before he was even close to the source of the magical crystals, a local sheriff spotted him and closed in to make the arrest. When the authorities returned to his cabin, they found all sorts of incriminating evidence of his illegal activities and, over the next couple of days, discovered his moonshine stills. They even found his favorite located near the Pyramids of Dan.

John Dudley would have gone to jail, had the judge not declared him stark, raving mad and institutionalized him. Now, he sits in his room every day, looking at people that no one but him can see. Sometimes he scrambles across the floor looking for the invisible pieces of his cross. The doctors and staff of the sanitarium report that the only words he ever utters are "I can't give it to you until I find it! I can't give it to you until I find it!"

When the residents of Martinsville tell this tale, they warn the listener to remember the fate of Little John Dudley. "Should you ever discover an eight-pointed fairy stone crystal in and around Bull Mountain plateau," they say, "don't wear it around your neck unless you intend to wear it for the rest of your life."

And the Earth Shall Have Them

And the Earth Shall Have Them

Carpenter and cabinetmaker Jeremiah Rowe hadn't treated his wife very well. In fact, over the last ten years, he had been a thoroughgoing cad. During his marriage, he had subjected his wife, Mary, to all manner of physical and emotional abuse, and now she was gone. She'd run off with a farm hand from Lynchburg, and as far as Jeremiah Rowe was concerned, he could have her.

Neighbors were silently on Mary's side in all of this. They'd seen Jeremiah take after her through the yard with his fancy cowboy belt. The belt had been a gift from his cousin in the Texas Territories out west, and its sterling buckle and fittings left wicked marks on poor Mary's arms and back. It was common knowledge that Jeremiah would drink whiskey as he worked on wagons, furniture, and coffins. By the end of the day, he'd be "angry drunk" as they say in these parts, and Mary would suffer the brunt of his mood.

There were many opinions among the farmers of Salem, Virginia, as to why Jeremiah beat Mary so badly and so often. Collectively, however, they decided it was because the Rowes were childless. Jeremiah blamed Mary for not bearing him any sons. "Yep," they said, "he showed his contempt by beating her, and she done run off." That's what the farmers would say when Jeremiah wasn't around, and he had encouraged their belief. The truth, it seemed, was much worse.

Jeremiah had been without his wife for almost a year. One day, as he was repairing a neighbor's buckboard wagon, he heard a strange sound come out of nowhere. He stopped working and looked around. "Who's there?" he asked. "Can I help you?" There was no reply, so he went back to work. Then he heard the sound again. The noise sounded something like scratching or whispering sounds that he couldn't make out. Jeremiah listened intently for a few moments and decided that it was coming from the wagon box behind the seat of the buckboard. He hopped up on the back of the wagon and approached the box. The scratching sound got louder. "Darn varmints," he said. "They get into everything."

He lifted the lid of the wooden box expecting to see a rat or raccoon chomping on leftover grain. Instead, a decomposing hand covered in rotting cloth lunged up through the opening and clutched at his throat. A rasping voice screamed, "Let me out!"

At the gruesome sight of the hand reaching upward, Jeremiah fell backward onto the bed of the buckboard. As he landed, the wagon box lid fell shut. He lay there shaking, barely able to breathe. It was at least a minute

47

before Jeremiah got up. The scratching noise had stopped, so he approached the wagon box again. Armed with a hammer held high in his right hand, he flung open the lid of the box with his left. It was empty. Jeremiah Rowe stood perplexed, staring at the empty box. "I've got to quit drinking so much before noon," he said as he shook his head. Then he went back to work.

Later that afternoon, Jeremiah had all but put his hallucination behind him. He'd been drinking heavily all day, and now, in his usual fashion, he was good and angry. Sitting on his front porch, smoking his pipe, and watching the approach of twilight, he wished he had Mary around so he could take out his rage on her. "It's all her fault anyway," he said with a snarl. "If she had given me a son—just one son—all would be right with the world. But no, she couldn't even do that. Deserves what she got. Yes, indeed; deserves what she got."

Jeremiah stood up. It was time to eat the stew he'd prepared earlier. The stew had been on the stove for most of the afternoon and was probably just about ready. "Betcha my stew is better than anything that worthless woman could cook up," he said contemptuously. He took a deep breath and turned to open the door of his home. As Jeremiah swung the door open, a corpse confronted him, and it was reaching for his throat with bony fingers. "Let me out!" screamed the banshee.

The stench of decay pushed over him as dead hands clutched at his throat. He fell backward, stumbling over the three simple stair steps to his porch. When he hit the ground, the ghost and the stench vanished, and he found himself staring through the open doorway of his home. He gathered his wits through an alcohol-induced haze, stood up, and brushed the dust off his clothes. Jeremiah couldn't help thinking that there was something important and oddly familiar about his vision. Then it hit him. The corpse was a woman. Not only that, but it was wearing the same kind of dress that his wife had been wearing the day that she ran off, or, more precisely, on the day that Jeremiah had killed her.

It was almost a year to the day that Jeremiah Rowe had bashed his wife's brains in. He'd thrown her into a large wooden provision crate he was making for a family of pioneers. At the time he'd buried the makeshift coffin, he said, "This box was supposed to go out west, but now it's taking you straight to hell." As he threw the first few shovelfuls of earth onto the crate, he could hear his wife pleading with him to let her out. Jeremiah buried her alive and never looked back. Now, it appeared, she'd returned from the grave.

He was trying to decide if the ghost had come back to haunt him or avenge herself. "Can I be rid of you, woman?" he yelled at the empty rooms of his house.

"You're dead and buried! Stay that way! Leave me alone!" Jeremiah searched his house from one end to the other, shouting invectives and insults at thin air. "Come out and face me, you ghost! You don't scare me!" But his courage was, for the most part, liquid, and, as he began to sober up, Jeremiah Rowe became terrified.

"What am I going to do?" he muttered. "You're dead! I killed you myself." With shaking hands, he poured himself a stiff drink and threw it back. The burn seemed to clear his head. Then he had a flash of what he must do. "By God," he said, "I'll dig you up and make sure you're dead!" Jeremiah resolved to unearth Mary's body and burn it to ashes. The field where he'd buried her was remote enough that no one should be the wiser. He gathered up a pocketful of matches and went to the barn to hitch up the horses and get a shovel and some lamp oil.

As he threw open the barn doors, Mary's ghost in a bloody and tattered dress lunged at him, screaming, "Let me out!"

This time, Jeremiah stood his ground in the opening of the barn and took several furtive swings at the wraith. His fists met only air, pushing through the apparition. "You can't haunt me, woman—you're dead!" His words echoed all around, but the ghost was gone. He hitched a team of horses to his wagon and headed off to a secluded open field on the outskirts of Salem.

Jeremiah had no trouble finding the spot where he'd buried his wife. He stopped about twenty yards away from the exact site. "No horse can tolerate a corpse," he thought. He hopped down from the buckboard and secured the shovel and lamp oil. He pulled out a match, lit a lantern, and headed off toward the hidden grave.

As he got closer to the site, he kept hearing Mary's voice, pleading to be let out of the wooden crate. Her cries, mocking him, rose up from the very earth itself. "Shut up, damn you!" he demanded. The pleading stopped suddenly—in fact, everything went silent. The sounds of frogs and crickets, even the sound of wind, vanished. The sudden silence stopped Jeremiah in his tracks. He held his lantern up to survey the field around him.

He should have been looking at the field beneath his feet. All at once, dead hands and arms thrust up through the ground and seized Jeremiah by his legs. He shrieked and dropped his lantern. The skeletal hands began to drag the woodworker down into the ground. He clutched at the grass and ground around him as he continued to sink into the field. He felt stones scraping against the flesh of his chest. Soil pushed up around his face, engulfing him, and began to fill his mouth. He tried to scream, but passed out as his head was dragged completely beneath the surface of the field.

Jeremiah woke with a start. He was relieved that he wasn't covered in earth. He rubbed his face and took a deep breath. "Thank God," he said aloud, "it was only a nightmare. I've got to quit drinking so early in the day." It was then that his hand brushed up against a cold wooden surface. He began to reach out all around. But no matter which direction he chose, he felt only cold, moist wooden walls. Then he realized he was in a confined space.

"What's going on here?" he said. Jeremiah reached into his pocket and grabbed a match. He took it out and struck it with his fingernail. As the match flame cast its glow all about, Jeremiah Rowe saw that he was in a large wooden provision chest, in fact, one made by his own hand. He turned his head and saw the rotting corpse of Mary Rowe lying next to him. Her lips were curled back in a ghostly grin. Jeremiah screamed and dropped the match. Blackness engulfed him. He pounded at the walls of the chest, but the earth that he himself had packed around it almost a year ago held firm.

Several other people over the years have completely disappeared when walking through the open field where the Rowes supposedly lay buried. To this day, residents of Salem will listen intently when frogs and crickets cease their nocturnal chatter. In the silence, they say, you can still hear Jeremiah Rowe pleading against the night. "Let me out," his voice says, "please let me out."

The Bridge of God and the Night of the Demon

The Bridge of God and the Night of the Demon

"You can't go back there," the old man said. "The spirit of the cave will kill you." But Michael Edward Larkin, geologist, was not about to be put off.

"I have to go back," he replied. "My journals, samples, and measurements are still by the pit."

Larkin's companion shuddered when the pit was mentioned. "It's on you, then. I wash my hands of it, wash my hands completely." With that, the old man quickly left the barroom.

Michael killed the last of his whiskey and pondered his next move. He and the gentleman who was walking out the door had been two members of a party of spelunkers who had been hired by Colonel Henry Chester Parsons to explore a cave located on two hundred acres of land northeast of Roanoke, Virginia. Colonel Parsons purchased the land some years earlier in 1881 and had turned parts of it into a colonial tourist attraction.

The main attraction was the natural bridge, a 215-feet-high stone bridge connecting the Blue Ridge Mountains with Short Hill Mountain. It was a unique combination of limestone formations, an ancient stream, and millions of years that had created this natural wonderland. Waterfalls, small creeks, and streams inside pools infused the whole area.

George Washington had been the first person to survey the bridge and surroundings. He even carved his initials on it. But another founding father, Thomas Jefferson, was the first owner of this beautiful and mysterious property. Rumor has it that he thoroughly explored the area, discovering many strange animals and witnessing strange events too frightening to retell. This was, indeed, a place of great wonder and natural power, and that's what drew the tourists.

Colonel Parsons operated two excursion trains that brought hundreds of people to his attraction. The entrance fees to see the bridge were nominal, and folks came from all around to stay at his hotels and eat at his restaurants. Some stayed all summer. Everyone in the area profited from the Parsons Natural Bridge. Local farmers sold food, while craftsmen, cooks, and wagon drivers tended to the needs of the guests. It was a very successful venture by anyone's standards.

It was the success of the bridge as a tourist attraction that inspired Colonel Parsons to explore Buck Hill Cave located about a quarter mile to the west. Michael Larkin knew just how beautiful and amazing a place this cave was. His team of explorers had been hired by the colonel to map the cave. His fellows were the most highly skilled spelunkers and cave explorers that could be found, and Colonel Parsons wanted a thorough study of the cave. His intention was to develop the underground world inside Buck Hill Cave as another one of his tourist attractions. If everything panned out like the colonel thought it would, he was even considering moving an entire city underneath the surface of the ground. That, he believed, would be the ultimate attraction, and he would be rich.

The well-provisioned team of men set out on their expedition. Michael, as a geologist, took small samples of earth and stone along the way and made journal entries about the interior of the cave. It was an amazing place. There were cathedral-sized caverns, huge ceilings, and lakes that shined like there were multicolored gemstones underneath the surface of the water. The bodies of water they discovered were vast, large enough to put a boat in. Huge limestone formations were everywhere. Waterfalls inside waterfalls went up just as far as the eye could see, cascading down in a beautiful display. The caves were labyrinthine and moved in and out in all directions. They also seemed to keep going on and on forever.

But the team moved forward. They just kept going deeper and deeper into the cave and finding more and more amazing and wondrous scenes. Late one Friday afternoon, according to accounts, the team stopped to rest, and with their lamplights positioned properly, they decided to sit down and have dinner.

Off to one side of their campsite was a huge cavern, a gaping black hole. No matter how they shined their lights into the hole, they couldn't see the bottom. They could barely see the sides. It was just a large opening of blackness into the earth. They took turns throwing things off the side. They threw stones into the huge hole in the depths of the earth to find out if they could hear when the rocks hit the bottom. But the pit, it appears, was bottomless. They couldn't hear anything. No matter what they threw in, no matter how much noise they made, no matter what they did with their lanterns, noises they made, or ropes they lowered, they couldn't discover how deep the pit was. Someone even threw a lantern down into the hole. The lantern and its light just disappeared into the blackness. The team never heard it hit bottom.

The team turned away from the pit to continue with their meal. As the men were finishing up their dinner, they heard strange sounds coming from the black pit. They all stopped to listen. Gathering on the surface, they heard a multitude of sounds. Michael said, "What is that? What are we hearing?" No sooner had the words left his lips than the team of experienced cave explorers began to hear moaning coming from the black cavern. The more they listened, the louder the moaning got. Soon, the moans turned to groans as if from souls in torment. And then they heard angry, ferocious sounds emanating from the black hole.

Fear gripped the party, and they decided to gather up their stuff and move on. Then the groaning turned into a loud shrieking sound, like the sound of a wild animal. The ominous sounds got louder and louder. Then it seemed something was moving up from the blackness toward the opening of the pit where the men stood. In a panic, the experienced cave explorers grabbed what they could, leaving most of their tools, records, and everything else. They ran away from the pit and made their escape out of the cavern as fast as they could.

The team reported that as they were running to get out of the cavern to find their way back up to the opening of Buck Hill Cave, the groaning, shrieking, and growling sounds they heard continued to follow them and were actually pursuing them. It seemed as if some sort of large beast or wild animal was chasing them out of the cave. When they actually made it to the face of the cave, they quite literally threw themselves out of the opening and collapsed in exhaustion onto the ground. As they lay there, they could still hear the moaning and the shrieking. They didn't go back to get their equipment.

They didn't go back to get their records. They left everything, with most of the team members vowing never to enter the cave again.

Michael Larkin, however, had not made that vow and was determined to return to the cave to find his journal and samples. While Michael was leaving the barroom, he thought about the old man's warning about the spirits of the cave. But Michael was a rational man and not given to superstitious fright.

Later that week, as he stood at the opening of Buck Hill Cave, he gathered his courage and set off on his quest. As Michael penetrated the cave, retracing the steps of his original team, he listened intently for the unearthly moaning and angry shrieks that had previously driven them away. He silently vowed to leave the cave and never return if he ever heard those sounds again.

All was quiet as he eventually reached the gaping pit that had been the end of his previous journey. Michael deliberately avoided looking into the pit and set to work gathering his journal and sample bag. He was able to find everything he had dropped when the team made its hasty escape. He heard no eerie sounds. In fact, the air inside the depths of the earth was pregnant with silence. Then, for some reason he couldn't fathom, Michael Larkin crept to the edge of the pit and looked into the blackness. It seemed to swallow the light from his lantern.

But in the edges of the illumination, he noticed a swirling of vapor several yards below the edge of the pit. For the first time in his life, Michael had a waking dream. In the swirling mists, punctuated by tiny flares of phosphorescent light from the cave walls, he witnessed a scene of pitched battle. He saw savages striking each other with clubs and tomahawks. Then the scene shifted to show battlefield pandemonium as women and children ran for protection amid the rocks and forest. Michael identified the forest as the area around the natural bridge. Images of despair and slaughter floated within the opening of the pit. It looked as if the battle was about to end when a lone Indian medicine man appeared and stretched his arms wide.

Michael saw the ground shake and roll. What followed amazed as much as frightened him. In the mists of the pit, he witnessed the scene of the mountain at the forest edge shift and move as if it were alive. One huge section of rock began to jut outward from one rock face and move toward another. Michael was witnessing the creation of the natural bridge. Braves, old men, women, and children dashed across the bridge to the safety of the rocks and caves with their enemies in hot pursuit. Again the medicine man gestured with outstretched arms and summoned the most horrific beast Michael could image. It was a huge ghostly phantasm with teeth, claws, and eyes that burned like coal. The creature descended on the pursuers, eating their very souls. Dead husks that had been warriors fell to the ground in and around the natural bridge.

With a shriek, the phantasm turned and plunged into the earth. With a fear growing inside him, Michael exclaimed, "Oh, my God! It's returning to this very cave. This is where the creature lives. I'm in its home!" The vision ended abruptly. Michael stared into the blackness of the bottomless cavern, unable to move … until a loud shriek broke his trance. He heard screams and cries of torment emanating from the rock walls all around him. They were the screams of the victims devoured by the thing in the pit.

Then he saw it: two red eyes moving upward toward him from the blackness. As they got closer, he clearly saw the snarling phantasm with its gaping maw and claw-like hands. Michael Larkin ran for his life.

It seemed an eternity before he emerged into the daylight. His chest heaved in the fresh air as his body ached from exhaustion, but he was alive. As Michael's wits began to return, he realized that he had again dropped his journal during his latest escape from the cave. A distant scream echoing from the opening of Buck Hill Cave told him that, as far as he was concerned, the journals were lost forever.

~

Native American legend tells stories of a mystical tribe called the Monacan. For many years, the Monacan had been hunted and persecuted by the Shawnee, who drove the Monacan to near-extinction. At the tribe's darkest hour, the Monacan entered a strange and mysterious forest in an attempt to elude their enemies, but the Shawnee soon caught up with the them, and the final battle commenced.

When it seemed that the Monacan were trapped against a mountain face, the tribe's medicine man called upon his powers to summon the Great Spirit. The ground shook and a stone bridge appeared from the mountain and allowed the Monacan to make their escape. The Shawnee, however, would not be denied and followed them onto the stone bridge. Then, with another wave of his hand, the medicine man summoned a huge horrific beast from the depths of the earth. The demon ate the souls of the Shawnee and carried them back to the bowels of the earth to spend eternity in torment. The Native Americans in the area still refer to the rock formation as the Bridge of God and the events that transpired there as the Night of the Demon.

~

Colonel Parsons died of a gunshot wound in 1894. He had been a victim of murder. There have been other owners of the natural bridge tourist attraction, but none of them were able to meet with the colonel's success.

There have also been several attempts to commercially develop the area in and around Buck Hill Cave, but each was stopped for one reason or another. Some developers say that strange subterranean air currents create strange noises around the cave. Some even report the sounds of moaning as if a person was in pain, or voices shrieking in anger as if someone is speaking or yelling at them. Some even report hearing the sounds of a large animal, the same kind of animal that must have chased the original explorers out of the cave. To this day, no one knows what lives under the ground in Buck Hill Cave, but whatever does live there, it's clear that it doesn't want to share its space with anyone from the surface.

Grace: The Witch of Pungo

Grace: The Witch of Pungo

All manner of witchcraft is practiced in old Virginia. In fact, even more than Puritan New England, Virginia was rife with practitioners of the black arts. Throughout the nation's early history, some even said that Satan's power visibly reigned in Virginia, more than any other place in the world.

That having been said, the authorities and residents of colonial Virginia had a much more relaxed attitude toward the practitioners of witchcraft than their New England counterparts. By and large, they accepted practitioners of the magical arts as something of an unfortunate inevitability. But they also knew that obliterating witchcraft altogether from the colony would be next to impossible. As in its sister commonwealth, colonial Massachusetts, Virginia, too, had its witch trials.

Almost anyone could be accused of being a witch or warlock. If you were too tall, too short, too attractive, left-handed, or had prominent features different from those of the community around you, you could be charged with being a witch. The records of the time detail the trials of many who were falsely accused of witchcraft. In 1622, Goody Wright of Virginia was accused of casting a spell on a young family. Soon after the couple's first child was born, the young family experienced a run of bad luck and accused Goody of casting a malevolent spell upon them. Now it appears that Goody Wright did indeed have some psychic abilities, such as precognitive sight and the ability to communicate with animals. But the sole ground upon which she was arrested and accused of witchcraft was based on the fact that she was left-handed, an anomaly at the time.

Local folklore abounds with descriptions of witches meeting in small—and sometimes large—covens and dancing in the moonlight. One old-timer said, "Oh, yes, witches dance. I've seen 'em! They dance and can put the hex on you no matter where you are. It's best to stay clear from the witches on the Sabbath."

As in Massachusetts, accusing someone of being a witch became something of a local pastime. If anything bad happened to you, if crops failed, or if a horse or a mule got sick and died and there was no other obvious explanation to account for it, then witchcraft was automatically assumed, and the person upon whom the ill fortune fell began looking for a scapegoat. In many cases, those who had been falsely accused turned around and successfully sued their accusers after their acquittal. Malicious slander, it seems, was a much easier case to prove than was the charge of practicing the black arts.

69

This was the kind of history that had excited May Phillips her entire life. Ever since she had been a small girl growing up in Virginia Beach, she had been fascinated with the stories of Virginia witches and warlocks. Like most people in Princess Anne County, May was fascinated by the story of Grace Sherwood, perhaps Virginia's most famous witch. Conventional history tells us that Grace Sherwood was accused of blighting a neighbor's field in 1698. Over a period of years, suspicion about Grace Sherwood grew, and eventually county officials and local residents accused her of being a witch. History also tells us that she was quickly convicted, because she failed the most reliable test of the time to determine if someone was a servant of Satan. The practice was called "Witch Ducking" and consisted of tying the accused witch's thumbs to her big toes and dropping her in a body of water. If her heart were pure, God would come down and hold her beneath the surface of the water to prove her innocence. If, however, she were a servant of the Dark One, she would bob up to the top of the water, proving conclusively that she was a witch.

On July 10 of 1706, at the stroke of ten, Gracie Sherwood was bound according to tradition and thrown into the western fork of Lynnhaven Bay. To this day, it is known as Witch Duck Point. Sherwood, naturally, floated to the top, satisfying the hundreds of onlookers that she was indeed a witch. She was jailed for a time at the Ferry Plantation House, but was later released. Conventional wisdom holds that she lived out the rest of her days quietly and never practiced witchcraft again. She died in 1740.

At least, that is the accepted history.

May Phillips was not satisfied with common knowledge and conventional wisdom. She had made an in-depth study of the controversies and events of Grace Sherwood's very colorful life. What she unearthed in local records, old newspaper articles, and gleanings from local storytellers convinced her that Sherwood's power was truly great and that she had never given up the practice of witchcraft.

As it turns out, according to May, Grace Sherwood was a woman ahead of her time. She was attractive and intelligent and not content to be a protected wife. She wore men's clothing, worked in the field, rode horses, and spoke her mind often. This seemed not to bother her husband, James, who was more than happy to share the many tasks around their farm that were usually reserved for men folk.

The breeches, riding boots, and ruffled linen shirt that Grace wore showed off her ample figure, much to the horror of other wives living in the area. Such behavior was unseemly and scandalous to her more matronly neighbors. But Grace delighted in making them uncomfortable. She would send anonymous notes to them and would secretly take things from their property only to return them later. Grace was a practical joker and could never understand why her victims all took themselves so seriously. The Witch of Pungo was also a skilled midwife and an expert in herb lore. She could combine roots, herbs, and berries to suck the poison out of a wound in no time. She could prepare poultices and lotions for a variety of ailments, but it was her magical skills that made her infamous.

May discovered reports that Grace Sherwood had been seen literally floating above the treetops near her home. She had even been caught teaching a local girl how to fly on a broom. One night, a pair of woodsmen startled Grace while she was apparently performing the witch's Sabbath. At one glance from the Witch of Pungo, both men were struck blind for a day. It was even rumored that the witch could transport herself across the ocean to England or Ireland, bringing back whatever she needed to make her magic potions.

May Phillips could still remember the very first time she heard an old storyteller spin the yarn about Grace Sherwood and the herb rosemary. Needing the fresh herb for a magical potion, Grace shrunk herself down to the size of a coin and then, so the story goes, transported herself in a hollowed-out egg across the ocean to England. There she secured fresh rosemary and packed it into the egg. She flew back to Virginia in the blink of an eye, grew back to normal size, and proceeded to make her potions. Local legend holds that rosemary grew nowhere in North America until the Witch of Pungo brought it here.

Sherwood had the ability to change herself into a cat, a raven, a dog, a wisp of smoke, and even a spider. With these powers, the old-timers said, she was able to keep an eye on the residents of the little town of Pungo. It was in these various forms that she was able to eavesdrop on them and learn of their malicious slander against her. Time and time again, Grace Sherwood would sue her neighbors for this crime, and more often times than not, the court found in her favor.

James Sherwood died in 1701, and the tide changed for the worse for Grace Sherwood and her three sons. Several years later, Grace sued a local woman who had been spreading the "rumor" that the witch had cast a spell on her. The court was indifferent to the charge and, even though they found in favor of the widow Sherwood, awarded her only twenty shillings in damages.

73

Charges and countercharges flew. Reports of supernatural activity in the small community increased almost exponentially. Ghosts of the dear departed were seen wandering aimlessly throughout the countryside. Strange lights were seen floating in the trees. Cows stopped giving milk, and prize bulls seemed unable to perform their duties. One of the stories that May Phillips liked most of all was the report that Grace Sherwood had turned a local busybody into a horse. The woman in this case described in detail how Grace Sherwood had floated through the keyhole as a wisp of smoke and transformed herself into a black cat. Then, with a swish of her tail, she transformed the old busybody into a horse, jumped on her back, and rode her through the countryside all night long. When the old woman awoke the next morning feeling uncharacteristically exhausted after a long night's sleep, she miraculously remembered the bewitchment and attributed it to Grace Sherwood.

Shortly thereafter, the busybody found herself the forewoman of a jury whose job it was to declare the guilt or innocence of Grace Sherwood, who had been brought up yet again on formal charges of witchcraft. While women did not normally serve as jurors in colonial Virginia, in the case of witchcraft, local women were frequently asked to sit in judgment of another woman. As far as May Phillips could determine from her research, this entailed a thorough examination of the body of the accused, something a man would never be allowed to do. A tell-tale sign called Satan's Mark would be somewhere on the body of the suspected witch indicating that she had made a pact with the devil. In the case of Grace Sherwood, two moles on her privates condemned her. It was in support of this accusation that the county court ruled that she must further be judged by ducking. Before they threw Grace Sherwood into the bay, she cursed the townspeople, telling them that they, too, were going to get the ducking of their lives.

After Grace floated to the surface of the water, proving once and for all that she was a witch, the townspeople retrieved her and took her to jail. Along the way, the beautiful summer sky rapidly darkened over with thick clouds. Thunder and lightning crashed. Then the heavens opened up, and a flood like none ever witnessed before began to punish the townspeople leading Grace away to jail. They were blinded by the deluge and tripped in the mud of the flooded roads. Even the wind, as the stories go, sounded like angry dogs and demons nipping at Grace's persecutors. Grace Sherwood just laughed throughout the event.

May Phillips chose to regard all of these tales as whimsy. To her, Grace Sherwood was one of our nation's first liberated women and was made to suffer for it.

Colonial Virginia had no place for a woman who spoke her mind and made her own way in life. The shortcomings and weaknesses of others, May thought, would always be displaced onto the strong and confident.

Once she was released from prison, Grace Sherwood supposedly led a quiet and uneventful life. But May's research provided her with enough evidence to suspect that the Witch of Pungo continued to work her magic spells on the residents of the small community. But what had she been doing for those years leading up to her death? No records, no stories could May Phillips find.

When Grace Sherwood died, it rained for seven days and seven nights. She had warned her neighbors that this would happen. The local residents feared that the witch's watery curse had returned for good. The earth gave up Grace's coffin on the eighth day of rain, and it floated on the runoff from the torrential downpour. Then the rain stopped. Her sons collected the coffin and buried her again. Once more, it rained for seven days and seven nights. Then, as before, the witch's coffin floated out of the earth.

Local legend has it that an area farmer discovered the coffin the second time. Atop the coffin quietly sat a black cat that just stared at the man. When the farmer approached the coffin, the cat arched her back and hissed, leapt off the coffin, and disappeared into the woods. Soon, the word spread far and wide that Grace Sherwood, the Witch of Pungo, was back. This time, she had transformed herself into a black cat. The residents were terrified. "We've gone too far," one man said. "We should have left her alone," exclaimed another. A handful of Pungo residents were so afraid they simply moved away, never to return.

May Phillips laughed when she thought about people being so afraid of a black cat that they would literally leave their homes and move away. But now as she sat on the ground next to Grace Sherwood's grave, she anticipated what was going to happen next. The moon was full and bright, and, as happens on every night of the full moon, cats from all over the city gathered at the witch's grave.

May came here often over the years. Tonight she even brought her own pet cat Grace (named after the witch) along with her. It wasn't long before the felines all began to howl at the bright moon. May's kitty joined in. A few moments later, a thin wisp of smoke crept up from the ground of Sherwood's grave and took the form of a large black cat with emerald green eyes. The ghost cat stared at May, but neither was startled—or even surprised—for they had met many times before. Soon, the ghost of Grace Sherwood in the form of a cat was singing along with the rest of her feline companions. As they sang, the cats gathered around a young girl who knew well the importance of being a strong woman and making her own way in life.

May Phillips just smiled and enjoyed the music of the night.

Ghosts of Confusion, Ghosts of Despair

Ghosts of Confusion, Ghosts of Despair

Of all the places he had visited during official Boy Scout outings, Billy Smith was enjoying this field trip the most. Colonial Williamsburg had a magical feel to it, and Troop 16 was having a ball. "The crown jewel of the Old Domain," thought Billy. The scout was thoroughly enchanted by everything he saw.

The scouts had done a little research in preparation for this excursion, but by and large, almost everything they saw was treated like a complete surprise. Well-chaperoned teams of uniformed boys on foot crisscrossed the historic section of town. Billy was with Mr. and Mrs. Culpepper, both of whom taught high school history. The Culpeppers' team was driving down Penniman Road about a half mile east of town. Mr. Culpepper was intending to tell the boys in great detail about the Battle of Williamsburg, one of the bloodiest chapters of the American Civil War. Little did he know that the teacher was about to become a student.

The only official reminder of the battle is a small stone monument nestled among a few trees. It became visible to the scouts in the car after they had traveled about a mile and a half down Penniman Road. Mr.

Culpepper parked the car, and the entourage got out and headed toward the stone marker. As they drew near the monument, Billy got a little lightheaded. He stopped a few yards away from the stone tablet and rubbed his eyes. "Mr. Culpepper," he said, "I'm starting to see things."

"What is it, Billy? What do you see?" the man asked.

"I feel cold, sir, and the grass … oh, the grass feels wet," Billy replied. It was the middle of the day on the first of August and anything but cold and wet in Virginia. In fact, it was so hot that Mrs. Culpepper thought Billy might be suffering from sunstroke.

"Sit down, Billy," she said and then sent one of the other boys back to the car to get some bottled water. But Billy wouldn't sit down. Instead, he took a few more furtive steps forward. As he did, sights that only he could see appeared before him.

"Where did all those trees come from? They weren't here a minute ago," Billy said. "Wait a minute," he added, "it's starting to rain." Billy's companions looked around. It was sunny. It wasn't raining, and there wasn't a cloud in the sky. Then the Boy Scout froze and looked off into the distance. "There are soldiers in the woods. I, I see people moving amongst the trees. Lots of them! They're covered with mud. I, I can't tell … they're so dirty. Are they Confederates or are they Federals? Now they're shooting at each other!" Billy stumbled back a couple of steps. "It looks like they've been fighting for days," Billy said. "I can see bodies laying everywhere; laying behind trees ... out in the open. I, I—I see bodies on top of bodies!"

Mrs. Culpepper started to get afraid. But Mr. Culpepper was listening intently. It was becoming apparent that Billy Smith was seeing the Battle of Williamsburg. The rest of the scouts listened intently.

"I can't believe how fiercely they're fighting," Billy said. "Wait a minute! They've completely run out of ammunition. They're using their rifles and bayonets as clubs and spears! It's starting to rain harder—it's starting to rain harder!"

"They all look so tired, Mr. Culpepper," Billy said, "and they're all so young. They're not much older than we are." The scouts standing around Billy considered how horrible it would be to fight a war at their age. Yet, the war that pit brother against brother had taken children for soldiers as well as young men.

Billy took a few more steps toward the monument. As he did, he began to describe detailed scenes of discouraged and confused soldiers. He told his companions of fierce hand-to-hand combat. "Look! Look!" Billy said. "There are soldiers just wandering through the bushes and trees like they're in some kind of trance. They're everywhere. They're all around us!"

Billy's words were filled with so much intent that Mr. and Mrs. Culpepper and the scouts were forced to look around to see if indeed there were any wounded soldiers wandering about. But then the young scout began to speak, and all eyes were on Billy.

"They're hiding. They're hiding in the bushes. They're hoping to hide until the war is over, until the battle is over. Where are the generals? They don't know what to do. They're confused. Some of the soldiers are just lying down because they're so tired. They're lying down to go to sleep, but they just die instead."

Then Billy pointed to the horizon. "Look! Look over there! Civilians! There are townspeople gathering on the edge of the battlefield." The scouts looked around, but only Billy could see what he was describing. "They're actually standing under umbrellas! There're some of them with blankets out on the ground … and picnic baskets! Look! There're carriages and horses everywhere … and servants helping their masters. They've come out to watch the battle like it was some sort of football game! I even see somebody trying to sell copper pots and someone else trying to sell newspapers."

The other Boy Scouts laughed nervously.

"How can they do that?" Billy asked. "How can they sit here and watch all of these people die like it was some sort of sport? There are actually people having

picnic lunches while men lay dying not far from them."
Then Billy described the sound of cannon and gunfire.
But he needn't have bothered; his companions heard it,
too. In fact, the sound had been so loud that Mr.
Culpepper had lost his balance, kneeling next to Billy.

"There're guns everywhere," Billy said, taking several
more steps toward the monument. "Can't you hear them?
Can't you smell the smoke? Listen ... listen! That's the
sound of sabers clashing one on the other. There's a
sword fight going on right over there!" Billy pointed to
an empty patch of ground.

Mrs. Culpepper shook her head. She actually was
able to hear the sound of sabers clashing together.
"What's going on?" she thought.

"Look! Over by the monument," Billy said. "There's a
Confederate soldier—there's a real Confederate soldier.
He's hiding behind the monument. Oh, no! The sounds
of guns and horses have scared him off!" Billy then sent
chills down the spines of his companions by letting out a
loud Rebel yell.

The young scout went on to describe a badly
outnumbered group of Confederate soldiers running
directly into a larger group of Federal soldiers. He
described how they charged headlong to their deaths.
"Oh, no!" Billy said. "Look!" And he took a couple more
steps forward. "The civilians got in the way of the

soldiers. Now they're being sucked into the battle! I see carriages burning and men and women from Williamsburg covered in blood. The Rebels are leaving now," Billy said. "The tide of battle has turned."

The scout took a few more steps toward the monument. His companions followed, listening intently. "The Union forces are taking control of the battlefield," Billy said. "It's getting dark now. They're not even bothering to pick up their dead. There are so many dead. Twenty, sixty, a hundred bodies stacked in one pile."

Then Billy looked at the monument. "There's that Rebel soldier again—he's hiding behind the monument. Can't you see him?" Billy asked. "He keeps moving from tree to tree and then behind the monument as if he's trying to hide from us. But I see him!" Billy walked closer to the monument, now just one yard from it.

"What's your name?" Billy asked the ghost. "Where are you from? My name's Billy Smith. Oh, don't worry; this is a Boy Scout uniform. I'm not in any army. What? What's that you said?" the scout asked. "Oh … I see. Your name's Billy, too." The exhausted scout closed his eyes and collapsed to the ground in front of the monument.

Mr. and Mrs. Culpepper tended to him instantly, pouring water over his face, head, and neck in an attempt to cool him off. When Billy came to, he filled them in on more details of what he had witnessed. As he continued to talk, Mr. Culpepper realized that the boy had indeed witnessed the sights and sounds from the original Battle of Williamsburg. Within about an hour, Billy had almost returned to normal, albeit a little subdued.

That night, as Billy prepared for bed, Mr. Culpepper came and asked him if he thought he was going to be all right. Billy said, "Yes sir, I think I'll be okay. It was just real hard seeing all those people die."

"I know," said Mr. Culpepper, adding, "but you have to remember the Battle of Williamsburg took place a long time ago, and it's over now."

"But you're wrong, sir," Billy told him. "The battle will never stop. It's frozen in time. That's what I saw, sir; that's what Billy told me. The battle never stops—it's frozen in time. The Battle of Williamsburg just goes on forever."

The Ghosts
of Swan Tavern

The Ghosts of Swan Tavern

"Oh, no, sir," said the antique dealer, "I couldn't take anything less than five hundred dollars."

"Come on, now," replied Bertram Nash, "five hundred dollars for an old painting with no verifiable pedigree? I don't think so." The men stood silent for a second or two as Bert studied the painting. The antique dealer kept a close watch on Bert's facial expression as he studied the old oil. Finally, Bert said, "Four hundred dollars."

The dealer scrunched up his face and counter offered. "Four fifty," he said, "and not a penny less."

"Done!" Burt shot back.

"Well, then, Mr. Nash, I'll just go wrap this up," the man said. "Why don't you look around some more and see if there isn't anything else you can't possibly live without." The two men smiled and Bertram Nash continued browsing the wares of the antique shop. The shop was housed in the old Swan Tavern in historic Yorktown. In fact, the painting he'd just purchased for a steal was a snapshot of the tavern and the colonial life that bustled around it. The Swan Tavern was the heart and soul of what had been called the most untamed township of the New World.

This was Bert's first trip to Yorktown, but he knew its history. The city was a busy port town, with everything that implies. Merchants, traders, colonists, and businessmen kept the money flowing through the town, while ruffians, highwaymen, and other less than savory individuals did their best to tap into it. Tobacco merchants, weary travelers, slavers, and criminals rubbed elbows with well-dressed gentlemen. And then there was liquor. Spirits could be cheaply purchased in colonial Yorktown. The Swan Tavern itself had seen more than its share of drunken patrons in its heyday. Many a drunken merchant had stumbled out of the tavern in his cups only to have a band of thieves cut his purse as well as his throat.

"It's hard to imagine those times," Bert said aloud.

"What's that, sir?" the antique dealer asked.

"Oh, just the whole wildness and violence of the place long ago," he answered.

The older man spoke up. "Well, now, Mr. Nash, this was truly an amazing place. It was the eighteenth-century equivalent of a fine hotel, a four-star restaurant, news outlet, theater, and sideshow all rolled into one. A weary traveler could experience more life here in a night than he could anywhere else."

"Then there was the part Yorktown played in the Civil War," he continued. "In fact, this building was used by the Union army to store gunpowder—well, not this actual building. This one's been restored. Someone set off the gunpowder in 1863 and the whole place went up— took most of this part of the town with it, too."

"Wow," said Bert.

"Yes," the dealer replied, "only left a couple of the original buildings standing. The blast and the fire afterwards destroyed this building right down to its foundation." The man smiled and added, "Things look pretty good now, though."

"That they do," replied Bert. It was then that Bertram Nash noticed a silver-tipped walking stick. "Hey, this looks good," he said.

The antique dealer chimed in. "Oh, that's a very interesting piece. It was actually dug up out of the ground a couple of years ago. I was having some work done out back, and a plumber unearthed it. It's in pretty good shape, considering."

For some reason he couldn't explain, Bert simply had to have it. The two men haggled back and forth for a few minutes and finally arrived at an acceptable price. Twenty minutes later, Bertram Nash was headed back to Richmond with his treasures. He had thoroughly enjoyed his weekend trip to colonial Yorktown and was leaving with two little pieces of its history. "It's been a good day," he mused as he motored down the highway. He didn't know it yet, but Bertram Nash was leaving Yorktown with more history than he could have possibly imagined.

Bert began to notice the strange occurrences in his house the very same week he hung the painting of Swan Tavern over his fireplace; however, he hadn't yet made the connection. At first, the events were just annoying. Small objects such as car keys, pens, and documents would go missing and turn up mysteriously in places that Bert never would have put them. Even his favorite antique briar pipe seemed to have a mind of its own and, one day, he "misplaced it" twice, only to have the briar show up once in the pantry and again, later, in his master bathroom.

"What's going on around here?" he said aloud. Then he answered himself: "I must be working too hard."

Bert replaced the pipe in its rack on the mantle. He glanced around the room to see if everything was in its place. Satisfied that all was as it should be, Bert walked out of the room. As he crossed the threshold, he couldn't shake the feeling that he was being watched. He stopped, turned, and surveyed the den again. His gaze fell upon the painting that hung over the fireplace, the painting of Swan Tavern.

Later that night, Bert was awakened by what sounded like voices coming from downstairs.

"Did I leave the radio on in the den?" he thought.

He put on his robe and slippers and proceeded down the long staircase of his two-story house. The strange sounds were clearer now, more distinct, and they were coming from the den. As Bert entered the room, he found himself confronted by a most perplexing sight. Sitting at the head of a large antique table in the den was a woman dressed in old European-style clothes. She gave the impression of being a gypsy, replete with a colorful bandanna around her head and large dangling earrings. It was clear by the tarot cards in her hands that she was engaged in telling a fortune, but for whom, Bert couldn't see. It was also clear that she was a ghost.

Bertram Nash watched transfixed as the ghostly soothsayer arranged her cards in the shape of a cross. She addressed someone else sitting at the table who Bert was unable to see. Then the gypsy arranged a vertical line of cards to the right of the cross-like formation. She turned to her unseen companion and spoke. "What's that?" she said in a thick accent. She paused for a moment and continued. "No, no, no—this isn't your fortune. It's his." With the utterance of that last word, the ghost turned her head and looked straight into Bert's eyes. Quickly, he looked down at the tarot spread on the table, but before he could see his reading, the cards and the gypsy simply vanished.

Bert turned on the lights in the den and nervously walked around, looking for anything that might explain what apparently was a dream. "No, no, not a dream," he muttered, "Something more than a dream, a vision, I guess. A warning of some kind. Oh, I don't understand." He stopped and rubbed his eyes, not knowing what really had just transpired.

A full month passed. Bert's memory of the spectral fortuneteller in his den had begun to fade. In point of fact, Bert had deliberately tried not to spend much time at all thinking about it. He had, however, spent a great deal of time staring at the painting of the tavern over his fireplace. He studied it in detail, examining every brushstroke and line and viewing it from every conceivable angle. All the while, Bert couldn't get over the idea that the painting might actually be staring back at him.

During one of his less-than-focused moments, Bert noticed that the painting's frame was in need of repair. It was only a minor repair, and one that Bert could easily perform himself. When he removed the painting from the wall, he heard a low moan come from behind him. Quickly propping the tavern painting on the mantle, Bert turned to see an antique armchair in the far corner of the den begin to rock back and forth. There was a palpable presence in the room. Bert could feel it. The armchair continued to rock on its own for over an hour before Bert decided to hang the painting back on the wall. As soon as he did, the rocking ceased. He turned, looked at the painting, and stepped backwards a few feet. Finally he understood: whatever was going on in his home was somehow connected to the oil painting. He continued to stare at it. Inexplicably, the painting stared back.

The next few nights were sleepless ones for Bertram Nash. Confused images of colonial life ran through his mind, making it impossible for him to get any rest. "It's that damn painting," he growled. Finally, he decided to put it away. "Maybe then I can get some sleep," he said. Bert went downstairs to the den and took the tavern painting off the wall. A few moments later, the painting was securely locked away in his attic, and Bert crawled back into bed.

Scarcely ten minutes passed before pandemonium broke out. All of the doors and windows in Nash's home were opening and closing of their own accord. Doors swung wide and then slammed shut with unearthly force. Windows moved up and down like machines until glass broke and sills cracked. Bertram was terrified. "The painting is angry," he thought. "I've got to put it back on the wall!"

He ran to the attic and retrieved the painting. Rushing downstairs to the den, he lifted it upward. As soon as the hook on the wall engaged the wire in back of the oil, the pandemonium stopped. Bert tried to catch

94

his breath. "What am I going to do?" he said. "Selling it is out of the question. If I got rid of it, the painting would probably tear the house down!"

It was then that Bert noticed something different about the painting. Something had appeared inside the painting, something that hadn't been there before. Peeking from behind the corner of the Swan Tavern was the painted figure of a man dressed in a dark hood and cape—a single gloved hand protruded from the folds of the cape and clutched at the edge of the building. Bertram began to shake: the cloaked figure was looking directly at him.

There were no nocturnal visitations for more than a month. But the passage of time had not eased Bertram Nash's mind. He found himself checking the hooded figure in the painting with an almost obsessed regularity. There it crouched, staring at him so intently that he felt the figure's eyes on him in every room of the house.

The following Saturday brought with it a powerful thunderstorm. Most of his neighbors had already lost electrical power, but Bert's generator kept his refrigerator running and most of his lights working. He was tending a fire in the den when he looked up and noticed that the painting of the tavern had changed yet again. The cloaked figure was no longer peering around the corner of the Swan Tavern. He was now standing in front of it.

Bert couldn't believe his eyes. He stepped toward the painting to get a closer look. In the time it took him to take those steps, the figure had moved again, this time toward the bottom edge of the painting. And then Bert noticed something else: the hooded man seemed to be getting closer.

Bertram Nash quickly backed across the room when, in the illumination of a flash of lightning, he saw the cloaked man crouching in the corner of the den. Bert screamed as the hooded figure stood fully upright and slowly moved toward him. Bertram wasn't able to move at all until he saw the large knife in the wraith's gloved right hand. Now he was able to move, and he ran for his life up the stairs to his bedroom.

Bert slammed the bedroom door and locked it. He ran for the phone on his nightstand to call the police. "I'll just report a prowler. That'll bring them here fast enough," he mumbled. But the phone line was dead. An eerie mocking laughter floated up the stairs toward his room and resounded against the locked door. "What am I going to do?" he thought. "How do I fight a ghost?"

He turned on his nightstand light to look around the room for a weapon of some kind. Then he noticed a silver-tipped cane resting on his pillow. It was the same cane he had purchased with the oil painting in Yorktown. "This is important," he thought, "it just has to be." Bert grabbed the cane and, brandishing it like a sword, threw open the door to his bedroom.

He moved to the head of the staircase and peered down through the shadows and partial light. He could see nothing, but continued to hear the cloaked man's sinister laugh. Then slowly the hooded man stepped to the foot of the stairs and looked upward. The pair stood motionless, one living and one dead, both locked in each other's gaze. Bert saw the ghost smile an evil grin and take the first step up the staircase. Two steps, then three steps, and then four. The ghost kept approaching as light flickered off his knife blade. By the time the ghost was halfway up the stairs, Bertram Nash had decided that he'd had enough.

"Get out of my house!" he screamed. And then he charged. Bert took one large swing with the silver-tipped cane as he collided with the oncoming figure. It felt as if he was passing through a wet sheet, but the ghost provided no resistance. Bert turned and looked up the stairs, but the ghost had vanished.

The power company restored electricity to the houses in Bert's neighborhood about an hour later. But even as he studied the painting in his den, Bert knew somehow that the worst was over.

~

In 1935, excavators discovered the skeletal remains of a man buried beneath the stables of the Swan Tavern in historic Yorktown. There was no way to determine the identity of the man, though it was assumed he had been a victim of foul play. One thing seemed clear though: an examination of the right leg of the skeleton revealed a badly healed break that almost certainly would have left the man lame, needing a walking stick to get around. No walking stick, however, was found at the time. Many people in Yorktown had seen the cloaked figure. A young Union officer even challenged the hooded man as he saw him skulking behind the Swan Tavern. When the figure refused to answer the soldier's challenge, the officer, with rifle in hand, ran to investigate, but the cloaked figure had vanished.

~

"Sometimes an artist can do too good a job," Bert wrote in his journal. "I don't know what to make of the events of the past month, but one thing seems certain: whoever painted the picture of the old Swan Tavern captured the very essence of the place, and, in doing so, bound forever the souls of those who lived and died in its shadow."

The Roman Ghosts
of Clarksville

The Roman Ghosts of Clarksville

Ruth, Carol, and Mary Evelyn had known each other for nearly twenty years. They met on the first day of elementary school and became friends almost instantly. Even now, on summer break from college, the trio behaved as if they'd met only yesterday.

The girls decided to spend at least one week together on their break and Carol's grandfather had the perfect place. He called it the camp, but it was more of a hunting lodge than anything else. It was nestled in the woods of southern Mecklenburg County and was the perfect retirement getaway for a professor of American folklore. The camp had everything that a person could want: spacious living quarters, a private lake, plenty of trees, and fresh air were the hallmarks of "the camp." However, its most important feature, at least to Carol's grandfather, was privacy. After years of teaching at a bustling university, the peace and quiet of the woods was what he cherished most of all. His old students still addressed him as Dr. Marshal, but Carol and her friends just called him Grandpa Ed.

Edward Marshal had made quite a name for himself during his career in higher education. He was an expert in Native American culture and language, as well as the myths and traditions of the earliest European settlers who made their home in Virginia. In fact, he had chosen to live in Clarksville specifically because of its strange legends and colorful history. These days, he spent his time and energy sifting through decades of research concerning the more obscure folk beliefs of Virginia. Truth be told, he was happy to host the girls' summer get-together. It broke up his routine in lake country and gave him the opportunity to visit with his favorite granddaughter.

The trio was relaxing on a floating dock about two dozen yards off shore when Ruth said, "Whew! Girls, this is a hot one."

"You can say that again," replied Mary Evelyn. "Who thought that sun-bathing could be such hard work?" The sounds of their laughter floated over the surface of the water.

"Okay, kids," Carol broke in. "It's time to turn over so we can get done on both sides."

"Forget it," Ruth countered, "I think it's time for a dip." With that, Ruth dove in to cool herself off.

Ruth swam leisurely around the floating dock. Periodically, she would disappear beneath the surface of the lake and swim under the dock. Ruth had been on the swim team in high school and was an old hand in the water.

Consequently, her two companions didn't feel the need to keep an eye on her. Carol and Mary Evelyn proceeded to doze off while she was exploring the lake solo.

Ruth was thinking about getting out of the water when something caught her eye. A ray of sunlight bounced off something shiny on the lake's bottom. She couldn't see anything the first time she dove down to investigate, but on the second try she spotted the object as it flickered in the sunlight. She swam to the bottom, made a grab for it, and snagged it the first time. Ruth was about to come up to the surface when, inexplicably, the object twisted out of her hands. She let it fall and came up for air.

"Hey, guys. I've found something," she said. "I'll be right back."

When Ruth bobbed to the surface, she held in her hand what appeared to be a cup of some kind. It had a wide flat base with sides that angled upward, making it look like a chalice. There was also something else: it shined like it was made of gold.

"Grandpa Ed should like this," said Carol. "He'll be able to tell us if it's a garage sale cast or something worth saving." With that, the girls weighed anchor and paddled back to shore.

Ed Marshal was in town when the girls got back to the camp. Early that evening, he walked in with enough groceries to keep ten college students happy. He placed the grocery bags on the kitchen counter and announced his arrival. "Carol, Ruth, Mary Evelyn, I'm back from the store. Who wants my world famous spaghetti and meatballs?"

"Hey, Grandpa," said Carol as she gave him a hug. "We found something we want you to take a look at."

The retired professor turned around and saw the goblet in Ruth's hand. In an instant, all thoughts of preparing supper were pushed from his mind.

"Where did you find this?" he asked anxiously.

"I found it at the bottom of the lake, just glistening in the summer sun," Ruth said happily. "We cleaned it up for you, too. And it looks like there's some kind of engraving around the base," she added.

Ed Marshal couldn't believe his eyes. What he held in his hands was almost a virtual impossibility. Just the thought of it made him hyperventilate. He knew that he had better calm down.

"All right. I'm getting ahead of myself," he said. "Let me get supper started, and then we can have a closer look at this thing."

"Do you think it's valuable, Grandpa Ed?" Mary Evelyn asked.

He replied, "I'm not sure, kiddo, but it will keep until after we've eaten."

The entire time that he was preparing supper, Ed couldn't get the goblet out of his mind. In the back of his mind, he suspected what it might mean but decided to keep his thoughts to himself.

When supper was finished and the kitchen cleaned up, the dinner companions sat down in the den to have coffee and hear what Grandpa Ed had to say about their find. In true professorial form, Ed had gathered a few old textbooks and a magnifying glass. He began to study the goblet intensely, jotting down brief notes in a journal every few moments. Finally, Ruth could take the sound of frantic scribbling no longer.

"All right, Grandpa Ed. Enough is enough," she said. "What's up with the golden goblet?"

"Well, first of all, it isn't gold," he said. "It's bronze, and a peculiar type of bronze at that."

The trio of girls just looked at him expecting the other shoe—whatever it was—to hit the floor.

Ed could sense their impatience. "Let me tell you a story," he said.

"In 1950, just east of here in Brunswick County, there was the discovery of two stone tablets about a mile apart from one another outside the small village of Dalton, Virginia. The stone tablets had some very unique inscriptions on them that, some students of archaeology say, are Roman in nature. Now, it wasn't the first time that this kind of thing has turned up in these parts. In fact, there have been several quite remarkable finds like this.

"In 1833, near Elizabeth, Virginia, workmen digging a well brought up a strange artifact from about thirty or forty feet into the earth. It was an oval-shaped coin about the size of an English shilling of the time. No one in the area could ever remember seeing anything like it before. There were figures on the coin, one representing a hunter and another representing a warrior of some kind, and other markings and writings that, according to historians, were of Roman origin. The people who found the coin or who handled it reported strange sensations in their hands and feet. They also heard sounds that seemed to accompany the coin wherever it went. The sounds were described as unearthly, or ghostly, sounds. Some even claimed that they saw figures in strange clothes when they heard the sounds."

"Wait a minute, Grandpa Ed," said Mary Evelyn. "What's the connection?"

Ed paused for a few moments and responded. "The writing on the stone tablets and the coin are just like the markings on your bronze goblet."

Everyone in the room was silent. Finally, Ruth got up to fetch the coffeepot. "Refills anyone?" she said. After she had poured the coffee, Grandpa Ed continued his story.

"There is more," he said, "a lot more."

With every word the old man sounded more like a professor lecturing his class than a grandfather.

"Right here in the small town of Clarksville, a farmer named James Howe made another discovery that only added more fuel to the 'Roman Ghosts of Virginia' fire. In the forties and fifties, James Howe gained notoriety when he unearthed evidence of ironworks in and around Clarksville. Now, the metal artifacts were unmistakably ancient in origin, but it didn't fit with any of the local records. There were no historical records of iron working by the local population, and the Indians who lived in the area didn't work with metal, either.

"But it was the nature of the metal artifacts discovered by Howe that caused a great deal of excitement. He discovered weapons of ancient design forged out of metal, including Roman short swords. He discovered odd chisels, hammers, and nails, and even a rudimentary form of threaded bolt, and a very sophisticated one at that."

Ed Marshal held up Ruth's goblet and said, "Probably the most important parts of the discovery, however, was a broken bronze goblet manufactured in an unmistakable Roman style. It was a goblet just like this one."

The three friends gasped and looked at each other in surprise. Before any of them could speak, Ed continued his narrative.

"The Smithsonian even got involved with Howe in 1951 and started a proper archeological dig in the area where the goblet was found. But they were beset by two problems. First, was a plan to flood the river near the dig site to make a reservoir in the area, so they had to work quickly. The second problem that hampered their efforts was the persistent visitation of spectral figures dressed in Roman garb—menacing figures. The more they dug, the more ghosts showed up and the more frightened everybody got. Then, the dig was cut short. Things got very strange for everyone involved when, all of a sudden, the officials at the Smithsonian unexpectedly terminated their involvement and decided not to carbon date the artifacts they had discovered. They also refused to return several selected artifacts from the dig. James Howe was, naturally, perplexed. He couldn't understand why they would back out of a project they had previously supported with great enthusiasm. Every Smithsonian official he spoke to about the decision nervously brushed him off. They seemed to be afraid but gave no clues as to what they were frightened of. Clearly, they were all hiding something, but Howe never found out what it was.

"Eventually, Howe petitioned other universities and specialists in carbon dating to examine the artifacts, but for reasons they wouldn't reveal, none of them would do it. To this day, the bronze goblet that he discovered is still property of the Smithsonian, but it is marked as 'Origin Unknown.'

"After the river was flooded and the reservoir established, there was, according to local legend, an increase in the sightings of men dressed in Roman garb throughout the area. This time, though, the ghosts were more menacing than they had ever been before."

It was getting late and the combination of the dark and the ghost story was beginning to spook the girls. They had no reason to suspect it, but Grandpa Ed was spooked as well.

"Did the ghosts ever hurt anyone?" Carol asked.

"Yes they did. At least according to the older folks that live in the area," Ed replied. "They even, from time to time, seem to be preparing for war."

"War?" exclaimed Ruth. "Who do they want to fight?" she asked.

"I guess they're mad at the people who flooded their land," Mary Evelyn said.

Ed broke in, "Near the old town of Springfield, which is now under water, Howe came across a formation of ancient stones arranged in the shape of a Maltese cross. These stones also had Roman style markings on them. Local residents would hear the sounds of primitive industry in the area, such as the beating of metal, the working of iron. They saw campfires in the area around the stone cross. Every now and then someone would gather enough courage to creep toward the fires for a closer look. But when they would get close enough to the mysterious campsites, everything would simply vanish. After the area was flooded, so they say, the Roman ghosts became very agitated and would hold war councils. One of those councils supposedly lasted for a month. Shortly after that, a party of hunters saw a small army of ghosts clothed in Roman attire marching in formation toward the deepest part of the surrounding forest. The area where they gathered before marching off is called 'The Barren Acre.' It used to be fertile ground, but now, nothing will grow there. The ghostly war council left it a dead zone."

Ed stared at the goblet that Ruth had pulled from the lake. He had previously regarded much of the story he recounted to the girls as backwoods fiction, but the bronze artifact he was holding in his hand made him wonder. How much of the tale was fiction, and more importantly, how much was the truth? He placed the goblet on the table that separated the den from the kitchen and went to locate another reference book from his library.

The conversation took a more mundane turn while he was out of the room. By the time he returned with the necessary volume, the three girls were talking about school, boyfriends, and a future skiing trip. Ed Marshal was gratified by the change in topics. "There's no need to scare them," he thought.

Thirty minutes passed before Grandpa Ed said goodnight to the trio. Though he enjoyed having them at the camp, their youthful energy made him feel old and more than a little bit tired. "No worries," he mumbled to himself as he went to his bedroom. "A good night's sleep will take care of everything."

Ed got up shortly after three in the morning and walked into the kitchen to get a drink of water. He switched on the light, took a glass from the cupboard, turned on the tap, and filled his glass. As he put the glass to his lips, Ed casually turned around to face the interior of the kitchen. When he completed his turn, Grandpa Ed came face to face with the terrifying visage of a Roman soldier in full battle armor. Startled, he backed against the sink and let out a scream. The sound of his drinking glass hitting the floor cleared his head enough to see that the soldier held something in each of his ghostly hands. In the soldier's left hand, he clutched Ruth's bronze goblet. In his right hand was the weapon that had conquered the world—a Roman short sword.

The jarring sound of breaking glass woke the sleeping girls.

"What was that?" asked Mary Evelyn.

"I don't know," replied Carol, "but I think I heard a scream!"

"Grandpa Ed, is that you?" Ruth asked loudly. Grandpa Ed couldn't hear her.

The three friends prepared to leave their room down the hall to investigate.

In the kitchen, the ghost of a long forgotten legion slowly raised his sword above his head. The soldier meant to strike down the old man who stood, trembling, in front of him. Before Carol and her two companions got to the kitchen, the phantom struck forcibly downward and a great blackness came up from the floor and swallowed Ed whole.

Ed Marshal woke up in a hospital room with the faces of Ruth, Mary Evelyn, and his favorite granddaughter hovering over him.

"Hi, Grandpa," Carol said. "How are you feeling?"

He couldn't muster the strength to speak. "Don't try and talk, yet, Grandpa Ed," Ruth said softly. "You've had a rough time."

"That's right," said Carol. "The doctors said that you had a heart attack. But you'll be okay now." Carol started to cry, and Mary Evelyn hugged her.

Ed squeezed her hand and drifted off to sleep.

~

The bronze goblet that Ruth pulled from the bottom of the lake had gone missing after that night. Everyone assumed that one of the paramedics or firemen had taken it, though no one could imagine why. The trio searched the house completely and even asked the neighbors if they'd seen it. But none of the neighbors could remember seeing a Roman-style bronze goblet with ancient writing on it. As far as Grandpa Ed was concerned, it was much better for them that they hadn't seen it.

A Ghostly Parade
of Homes

A Ghostly Parade of Homes

Author's Note

Some years ago, I led a team of psychic mediums and sensitives to investigate homes throughout the South that are inhabited by spirits of the dead—haunted houses. Our goal was to experience the full force of each spectral entity we encountered. Not merely interested in solving regional puzzles, we wanted to contact the poor souls that were drawn to these houses after their physical deaths.

A spirit can be drawn and bound to a specific site for a variety of reasons. They need not be related to the owners of the house, nor any earthly event connected to it. After death, however, the rules change, and a departed spirit can find itself forever joined to the living history of a house or building. Sometimes this binding occurs by choice. At other times, it doesn't.

Over the years, I've collected many stories of some of these ghosts and endeavored to piece together a picture of the spirit world that exists in a dimension parallel to our own. Think of these three stories that follow as a short ghostly Parade of Homes and a brief introduction to the spectral inhabitants that you can meet along the way.

One more thing: the homes described herein are by and large accessible to the public. Should you get the opportunity to visit these haunted houses, please stop and think about the ghosts that are part of its environs. I've described these spirits in as much detail as I was able to uncover. Let your mind rest on the details of their lives and personalities. If you are able to, as it were, relax into the idea of each of them, then they will surely appear to you. After all, in a moment, you will know many personal things about them. It seems only fair that they should become acquainted with you as well.

Dudley Diggs House

Location: The corner of Main and Comte de Grasse Streets, colonial Yorktown.

There are only two original wooden structures left standing from Yorktown's historic colonial period. One of them is the Dudley Diggs House. A white picket fence separates the house from the road. Four large windows and five gables frame the entrance to this quaint colonial home of Dudley Diggs and his wife, Martha Armistead Diggs.

A ghost can be seen walking the fence line in front of the house. He is a Frenchman by the name of Martin Beauchamp. As far as my team of investigators was able to discern, Martin found himself bound to the house after the death of Martha Armistead Diggs, who died in childbirth. In life, Martin had been a recluse who dwelled in the dark corners of Yorktown's underworld. He had lived a life of monetary riches, profiting greatly from his ill-gotten enterprises, but lingered alone in all other respects. It's this aloneness that, many suspect, binds him to the Dudley Diggs home. For no spirit was ever so alone as Martha Armistead Diggs.

Martha died giving birth to the family's second child. In fact, she left this world in the very same bed that her husband had entered it. The emotional impact of a young wife dying in the same bed that her husband was born in was too much for Dudley Diggs to bear, and he was bereft. Though he married again several years later, his love for his first wife never waned. Even in later years, Dudley Diggs spoke to the spirit of his dead wife, Martha, on a daily basis. He believed that if he thought about her often enough and strongly enough, she would forever remain with him in the house.

Dudley Diggs died at the age of sixty-two in the year of our Lord 1790. His spirit, however, moved on, but the spirit of Martha Armistead Diggs did not. Martin Beauchamp, bound to this home, witnessed the events that took place within its walls during the Revolutionary War. Dudley Diggs had been a close friend of Patrick

Henry, and the two used the home as a headquarters for fomenting rebellion against the English. The home became an important landmark of the Virginia revolutionary fervor.

Martin has witnessed the home being confiscated by British soldiers. He has seen it riddled with gunfire and damaged by cannon shot. He considers it a miracle that it was left standing at all. It was some time after Dudley Diggs's death that the spirit of Martha Armistead Diggs began to float in and around the house. Martin describes the frightful visage of Martha clad in a white—but bloodstained—nightgown floating from room to room in the house, weeping for her dead descendants. Visitors have seen her spirit in almost every window of the historic colonial home. More chillingly, she is heard weeping and sobbing, her sad cries emanating from the bedroom where she breathed her last. Whenever she is seen, she outstretches her arms, beseeching a passerby for aid and comfort. Whenever she is heard, she is heard pleading, pleading for someone to help her family.

It is true that the dead can affect the living. But the dead can affect the dead as well. In addition to being a criminal, Martin Beauchamp was also a warlock skilled in hexes and necromancy. In life, he'd been antisocial and was out for his own gains. He wasn't aware of how his actions affected the world around him. He became involved in witchcraft as a means of gaining power over his adversaries. More than anything, he wanted power, wealth, and control, and he wasn't afraid to intimidate or kill anyone who got in his way. But now, he finds a chance to redeem himself. If he can help the spirit of Martha Armistead Diggs, perhaps then he will be released from his servitude at their ancestral home. But to this day, he remains bound, unable to craft a spell that will release the spirit of the floating woman covered in blood.

As tourists file past the Dudley Diggs home, Martin watches carefully for anyone he thinks might possess the power or the skill to help him release Martha's spirit so that she may join her beloved husband, Dudley. In fact, several visitors who have leaned over the fence to get a close look at the Dudley Diggs House have reported hearing a voice speaking, in a thick French accent, the words "Are you the one?"

The Tayloe House
Location: Nicholson Street, Colonial Williamsburg.

The ghost of a dead patriot known only as Benjamin sits high on the rooftop of the Tayloe House overlooking its grounds. He stands tall, keeping watch over a huge encampment behind the house, but the encampment has long since vanished. The population of Williamsburg, Virginia, was part of the thousands who took up arms against the British crown in the late 1700s.

Independence, as history would record, was the quest, and those who did not support it were pariahs. Benjamin, however, had always longed for independence from the mother country, and he was one of the first colonists to lose his life in the struggle. Benjamin had been seriously wounded in the battle with Lord Cornwallis at Yorktown and had been removed to the Tayloe House so that his wounds could be tended. He died almost instantly upon arrival.

Colonel John Tayloe, who was a local justice of the peace, originally owned the house and grounds. Colonel Tayloe did not favor the patriot movement. He could not bring himself to, in any way, support their cause. The colonel lost his job and standing in the community, but unlike others who did not support the patriot movement, he did not flee to England for safety. Though he objected greatly, his house and grounds remained an important Williamsburg military encampment.

But the struggle for freedom does not die, and Benjamin, the sentry and protector, keeps watch over the grounds at Tayloe House. When he sees fit to communicate, Benjamin will tell you that he's itching for a fight. "The cause of freedom is just and noble," he says, and even in his ghostly form, his passion for freedom and liberty can take your breath away.

Nowadays, Benjamin keeps watch over reenactments of military exercises. Reenactors march and move in the footsteps of the real heroes of the Revolution. During special holidays, you can hear the sounds of actual cannon and gunfire on the grounds, as tourists imagine what it would be like to have lived during those historic times. But late at night, when the tourists have gone, ghostly cannon fire and the spectral sounds of troops talking and laughing can still be heard among the trees. And always, Benjamin the sentry is keeping watch.

Residents in the area who are fortunate enough to see him regard Benjamin as a protector of the community and their families. But he has revealed himself to only a chosen few. If you stand on the grounds behind the Tayloe House and look up toward the roof near the chimney, you can see the ghost of Benjamin the Patriot. Then, like so many of the residents of old Williamsburg, you may feel comfortable under his protective watch and ward.

The Coke-Garrett House

Location: Where Nicholson Street intersects Waller Road, Williamsburg, Virginia.

Three Confederate soldiers wander the house and grounds of the Coke-Garrett House. The clash of Confederate and Union troops in Williamsburg in 1862 turned this tranquil and idyllic community into a bloody nightmare. Many of the wounded were taken to the Coke-Garrett House for medical attention, and many died there. History records that during the battle, Dr. Robert Garrett tended to the medical needs of both Confederate and Federal troops. Amputated arms and legs were stacked in every corner of his surgery. Everywhere you looked, soldiers bloodstained the floor.

Two of the three Rebels who still inhabit the house and grounds had, in life, received amputations at the hand of Dr. Garrett. In death, however, they move about with arms and legs intact.

When they were alive, the three cared deeply about their freedom. They enjoyed coming and going as they pleased and were always ready for the next great adventure. Serving the Confederacy had been the greatest adventure they could imagine, and they were willing to risk their lives and sacred honor for the South.

But each was impulsive and reckless in his own way. On the day of their death, they ignored the orders of a superior officer, left their post, and encountered a superior Federal force. The battle was brief and deadly for the three. One of the three had actually picked up his wounded friend and attempted to surrender. Tragically, the rebel was shot by a Union officer at pointblank range.

Now, they play practical jokes on people who pass by the Coke-Garrett House. Visitors to the area often report seeing the spirits of dead soldiers walking on the grounds. But these three friends hide themselves until they spot someone they can annoy. Sometimes they will blow in a tourist's ear or pull the hair of little boys.

Such shenanigans, they will be delighted to tell you, are their way of letting people know that life is a great adventure and one that shouldn't be taken too seriously. These three ghosts choose to remain bound to the Coke-Garrett House so they may constantly remind us of the importance of freedom.

The Children
of Arlington Mansion

The Children Of Arlington Mansion

Susan Gray Eagle knew the price of freedom all too well. In fact, she had lost family members in World War II, the Korean War, and Vietnam. Now, as she walked among the graves and headstones of Arlington National Cemetery, the full impact of her ancestors' sacrifice hit home.

Susan was part Choctaw and part Cherokee. The Choctaw and the Cherokee, along with the Chickasaw, Seminole, and Creek Indians made up what was called, in the Civil War era, "The Five Civilized Tribes." Collectively, they represented the Cherokee Nation.

Susan's ancestors had been fighting in American wars since that time and continued to serve proudly to this day. Some of them were even buried beneath her feet in Arlington Cemetery. As she walked among the graves, she wondered aloud as she had so many times before. "What was it really all about?" she asked. "What was it all for?"

As a little girl growing up in Mississippi, Susan would listen to her great-grandfather tell stories about the Civil War and the part that Native Americans played in it. He told the stories exactly the same way every time. She was so familiar with them that she could recite her great-grandfather's words almost verbatim.

"In late October of the year 1861," he began, "the Cherokee Nation took sides in the Great War of Northern Aggression. The Choctaw, Chickasaw, Creek, Seminole, and Cherokee people sided with the Confederacy." It was at this point that Susan's great-grandfather recited paraphrased passages from the document that made the Indians' decision final.

"I quote now from the Indian document titled, 'Declaration by the People of the Cherokee Nation of the Causes Which Have Impelled Them to Unite Their Fortunes With Those of the Confederate States of America.' In this document, it is recorded that the Southerners disclaimed any intention to invade the Northern states. The Confederacy only sought to repel the invaders from their own soil and to permanently secure the right of governing themselves. They claimed only the privileges put forth in the Declaration of Independence, namely the right to govern themselves and the duty to alter their form of government when it becomes intolerable. These rights are the ones that even the Northern states are built upon.

"But the Cherokee people saw the Northern states violate their Constitution. The sight of this caused us great shock and alarm." The old man would then lift his head upward, close his eyes and continue. "The Cherokee saw the Northerners put all civil liberties in peril and the rules of civilized warfare discarded along with the dictates of common human decency."

The old man would continue to paraphrase the Declaration of the Five Tribes, making sure to emphasize the most important points.

"The states that followed the Union found their civilian powers replaced by a military authority and those laws established by the populace put down at the point of a gun. Free and truthful speech was declared to be unlawful. The president even set the military to control the highest court in the land. Soon he began a most hateful war against the Southern states.

"Now in the past, the people of the Cherokee Nation were not always the allies of the Southern states. However, the Great Spirit revealed to us that our destiny and fortune was intertwined with their own."

Again, he lifted his head and closed his eyes, saying, "The war that is now waging is one of Northern avarice and fanaticism. It seeks to annihilate the sovereignty of the Southern states and completely change, forever, the soul of government." With the close of his recitation, Susan's great-grandfather would call out in his native language, signaling the start of a larger ceremony. Then, those gathered tribe members would begin to sing. Susan found it strange that the songs were mostly Christian hymns sung in the Choctaw language. But as they danced in a circle as their ancestors had, Susan Gray Eagle wondered, "What was the war really about?"

Susan saw the first child while she was musing about her life. The tribal gatherings, the stories and traditions preserved by her family, life on the reservation, the music they played, and the songs they sung all faded to memory when she saw the little boy.

The child was dressed in out-of-date clothing and was standing with his back to a headstone some forty yards away. Susan might have not noticed him at all except for the fact that the young boy was waving at her. She automatically returned the wave. As she did, the boy dropped his hand to his side, turned, and walked away. Susan knew that kids would wave at just about anyone, so she didn't give it a second thought. That is, until she saw another child.

This child, too, was staring at Susan from about forty yards away. She wore an old-time play-party dress replete with petticoat. Susan was unable to get a better look at the child to see her face clearly, but she could tell that the girl had curly blond hair tied up in bright blue ribbons.

Susan was about to turn around and leave when the girl with the petticoat waved.

"What's going on here?" Susan muttered. "Have I walked into some sort of school field trip or something?" Susan Gray Eagle's words had barely left her lips when the little girl proceeded to walk off into the cemetery. For some unknown reason, Susan decided to follow her. Along the way, she looked at the graves, reading the names of the fallen heroes who were laid to rest there. Susan also noticed something else; the little girl had vanished completely.

Susan looked all around but couldn't find the girl. Then she remembered that she had been about the girl's age when she made her first trip to Arlington. Her grandfather was part of a tribal committee that was meeting with senators to discuss mining rights on the reservation. She remembered her grandfather saying, "If the South had won the Civil War, we'd have our own state by now, an Indian state."

Susan's grandfather had taken her to the Tomb of the Unknown Soldier in the early morning hours. She remembered that the grass was still wet with dew. She also vividly remembered the military Honor Guard marching back and forth at the entrance of the memorial. The guards, in dress uniform, moved with a hypnotic precision that transfixed her. She, quite literally, was unable to take her eyes off the tomb.

Susan and her grandfather had been silently watching the Honor Guard for about ten minutes when Susan had a vision. She'd heard about visions her entire life but had never experienced one—at least not one like this. She saw a spinning whirlpool of light and energy swirling around the Tomb of the Unknown Soldier. It seemed to reach out for her as if it wanted her to come closer. Instead, Susan grabbed her grandfather's pants leg and nervously stood her ground.

Later that night, she told her grandfather about the vision. "You have a gift," he said. "All of the women in our family possess this power." Then he leaned close, gave her a sly wink, and said, "Some of the men, too."

The next day Susan's grandfather took her back to the tomb and asked her to show him where the unearthly energy was strongest. Without hesitation, Susan walked to a small clearing near a stand of evergreens on the southeastern slope of a hill next to the tomb. Her grandfather laughed and said, "Yes, little one. You've got the sight, all right! Yes, indeed, you have the gift."

The truth was that Susan had not experienced another vision since that day. Now as a grown woman looking for a mysterious blond girl with blue ribbons in her hair, she wondered if she ever would again.

Susan walked over a small rise and noticed another small child standing a short distance away. Then she saw another girl she had never seen before. Yet another girl who appeared to be slightly older than the first appeared next to the other two. Almost in unison, the children waved gently at Susan, turned, and scampered away.

Susan quickened her pace in order to catch up with the kids, but as she came over the next hill, all three of the children were gone. For the first time in ages, Susan felt uneasy. She was wondering what to do next when she caught a glimpse of the children running toward a house on the cemetery grounds. She ran to keep up, but the children vanished somewhere near or into the house. Then she realized where she was. Susan was standing in front of Arlington Mansion, the former home of Robert E. Lee.

In all of her trips to Arlington, she'd never taken a tour of the Lee home, but a child's voice in the back of her mind urged her to do so now.

"Of all the beautiful antebellum homes of Virginia, Arlington Mansion is considered the most majestic," began the tour guide. "It was originally built by the adopted grandson of George Washington as a memorial to the first president of these United States. George Washington Parke Curtis had only one child, and in 1831, Mary Parke Curtis married the young and dashing Robert E. Lee. Robert was the son of 'Light Horse' Harry Lee, the famous hero of the Revolutionary War."

The tour guide was detailing the tranquil and idyllic life that Lee and his bride enjoyed at the mansion, but Susan was being distracted by something. Standing in the corner of the room was one of the children she'd seen earlier. The boy was playing quietly with an old toy horse and wagon. Oddly enough, no one else in the room seemed to take notice of him. The boy looked up at Susan and smiled. "Such a cute child," she thought.

"Robert E. Lee seemed destined to not remain here in his beloved home. In 1846 he left to fight in the Mexican War. Six years later he left to become the superintendent of the military academy at West Point. Shortly after that, the specter of Southern secession cast a cloud over the country and this house. After the war began, Federal troops seized the house and grounds to punish the rebellious general. At first, only Union dead were buried on this site, but in ensuing years, it became the final resting place for all of America's honored dead."

Susan wandered away from the group to find a place to sit down and rest her feet. She had little trouble finding an appropriate spot. As soon as she sat down, a purring cat hopped up in her lap. "Well, where did you come from, sweetie?" she asked. The cat closed her eyes for a moment as Susan began petting it. Then the little blond girl with bright blue ribbons walked into the room. Susan looked up for only an instant, but in that instant, the cat vanished. The disappearance seemed to occur in conjunction with a soft popping sound that startled Susan. When she glanced back up, the girl was gone.

Susan resolved to get back to the tour group. However, no matter where she looked, the group was nowhere to be found. She was about to go upstairs and look when a small boy came walking down the staircase.

He appeared to be somewhat agitated and brushed past Susan without looking at her or saying a word. In his hands he carried a teddy bear that was, obviously, his prized possession. Susan followed him into a room with a fireplace. The boy walked up to the fireplace and set the teddy bear in a small chair by it. The spectral child and his stuffed companion started to warm themselves at a non-existent fire. It was at this point that Susan Gray Eagle realized that she was looking at a ghost.

The faint sounds of voices caused Susan to turn around, but she could see no one. Then two more children came in to the room and joined the boy by the fireplace. "My God!" whispered Susan. "They're all ghosts."

Another child walked in, followed by four more. Soon more than a dozen ghostly children were in the room. Each quietly amused themselves. None spoke a single word.

Susan's head began to spin. One of the little girls noticed her distress and walked over to Susan and took her hand. Susan couldn't help but notice how radiant these children were. For the life of her, she couldn't imagine why they were all gathered in this house.

"Surely, you're all not relatives of the Lees, are you?" At that very moment, a stately woman with a dower look on her face marched into the room. Susan and the children watched as the woman walked over to the little chair by the fireplace and picked up the stuffed teddy bear. Then, she turned on her heels and marched out of the room, turned the corner, and headed for the stairs.

The ghostly children, with Susan in tow, followed the woman up the stairs to an opulent bedroom. Everyone watched as the woman put the bear on the bed, resting it against the pillows. The glower woman seemed to take no notice of either the living or the dead as she left the bedroom. The ghostly children waited until she was gone and began a silent giggle. Then they rushed to the bed and snatched the teddy bear. Susan and the children left the bedroom and headed down the stairs.

"Those little rascals," Susan thought, "are taking the teddy bear back downstairs to the fireplace."

Before Susan was completely down the staircase, she felt a sensation that urged her to go back upstairs. The little girl who was still holding her hand released it and smiled. She ran off to join her playmates by the invisible fire.

Susan walked into another bedroom off of the main hall. She saw the ghostly figure of a young and beautiful woman lying on the bed. It was obvious that the woman was ill. Suddenly, two more adults entered the room and stood over the supine form. One was a man dressed in the finery of a colonial country gentleman. He was weeping inconsolably, and it was obvious that the woman in bed was his wife. His female companion, however, did not display any emotion whatsoever. She spoke to the crying man.

"I wish I could hear what they are saying," thought

Susan. There was a strong physical resemblance between the two women, and Susan thought that they might be sisters. After a few more moments, the pair of ghosts walked past Susan and stood in the doorway of the bedroom. Unexpectedly, they embraced and kissed passionately. All sorrow for the dying woman had apparently vanished.

Just then, a man dressed in a ruffled shirt and long black coat strode confidently into the room. He clutched a ledger under his left arm. The man moved to the bedside of the sick woman and adjusted the blankets that lay over her. Susan was trying to get a better look at the ledger book under his arm when the man in the white shirt looked up at her. At first, Susan was frightened by the stern look the man gave her, but soon his frown melted into an amiable smile.

"Who are you?" she asked.

Much to her surprise, the man answered. "My name," he said, "is Light Horse Harry."

The sound of children playing diverted Susan's attention, and both of the ghosts in the room vanished with a soft popping sound. Just then, the phantom cat she'd met earlier hopped up on the bed. The animal's tail twitched furiously. It mewed a silent mew, and its actions clearly indicated that it was trying to get Susan's attention. The cat jumped to the floor and ran out of the bedroom with Susan close behind.

Susan crossed the threshold of the room to see dozens and dozens of ghostly children crowding every corner of Arlington Mansion. They were all young, healthy, and happy children. Some of them played with invisible toys while others read tattered books. Each one appeared content and peaceful.

"This is my family," a voice said. Susan turned back to the bedroom to see it filled with smiling children. In the center of the crowd stood the ghost of Robert E. Lee's father, "Light Horse" Harry Lee.

"You stand on hallowed ground, Susan Gray Eagle," he said. "Please come to the window and look out."

Susan walked to the second-story window and peered through it. What she saw took her breath away. The grounds around Arlington Mansion were covered by hundreds—maybe thousands—of ghostly children playing in the warm sun. They were everywhere.

The ghost of Harry Lee said, "I keep a record of them in my ledger, just so I can keep track, mind you."

Susan felt compelled to speak. "But why are they here?" she asked.

"Can't you guess?" replied Harry Lee. "Haven't you longed for a return to the simpler carefree days of your childhood? Well, some of my children have done just that. Others have found their way here to spend eternity in a constant state of wonder and playfulness."

He paused for a moment and continued by saying, "Still, others were brought here by their comrades. Those children are among my favorites."

"War is a terrible thing, Susan. It destroys innocence and steals youth. But sometimes it is necessary. When someone meets the challenge and pays the ultimate price, don't you think it's fitting they should get their innocence back as a reward?"

Susan Gray Eagle began to cry. Now she knew the answer to the question she had been asking for most of her life. The sacrifice that her family and so many others like them had made over the generations was for the children. And not just for the children that soldiers leave behind. The brave men who are buried in Arlington National Cemetery gave their lives to protect innocence and preserve the youth of others. They accomplished this by offering their own precious innocence and youth.

Just then, a National Parks employee tapped Susan on the shoulder to tell her that the house was closing for the day.

As Susan Gray Eagle walked out of the front door of Arlington Mansion, she caught sight of a small boy happily playing in the grass. He looked up at her, smiled, and gently waved. "It's all about the children," she thought. "It's all about the innocence."

The Phantom Train Wreck

The Phantom Train Wreck

Charles Dawes had worked for the railroad for most of his life. He'd done it all—laid track, repaired cross ties, and any other work that the railroad would pay him for. Over the years, Charles had worked his way up from "gandy dancer"—a railroad term for an itinerate laborer—to the enviable position of junior engineer. Mind you, he hadn't been given any important runs yet, but that would come in time. Charles was content to wait. He simply loved the railroad.

"The sound of a train whistle in the distance will set your soul free," he said. "Every time you hear a train whistle you know that a new adventure is beginning for someone. I always want that 'someone' to be me."

When he was younger he announced to his parents that he would be a railroad man. "Trains take people to places they have never been before," he told them.

As a young boy growing up in Virginia, Charles had dreamt of travel and adventure. A train, as far as Charles could tell, was the key to both. He was barely twelve when he hopped his first freight. Charles only went to the next town before getting off the train and heading back home. He made the return trip by rail, as well. It had only been a forty-mile trip, but it had been enough to seal the deal for Charlie. The railroad bug had bitten him. That night as he lay in bed, he made a child's vow to spend as much of his life on the rails as he could. Now, as an adult, he was honoring that vow.

Shortly after Charles became an apprentice engineer, a bridge near the small crossroads town of Cohoke started to cause problems. The railroad repairmen had tried their best to make the trestle secure, but every time a train passed over it, the rail bridge would shake and shudder. Charles had driven over the trestle several times in the last month and kept his senses alert for any additional signs of problems with it.

Charles got the word that someone on the nightshift had reported a loud creaking sound emanating from the bridge as the evening train passed over it. A repair crew had been dispatched but could find nothing wrong. Even though the repairmen had given the bridge a clean bill of health, Charles had serious misgivings.

Charles was due to take out his train shortly after dusk, and he left right on time. He thought about the bridge near Cohoke. "I'll have to be extra careful with that one tonight," he thought. He wasn't very worried, and after all, the Cohoke bridge was at least three hours away.

Charles was barely an hour into his run when he

heard a whistle blast come from somewhere in front of him. He looked ahead on the tracks and saw a light swinging back and forth in the distance. The conductor's gong sounded in his cab, and he applied the brakes.

The conductor ran up alongside the train and yelled, "Hey, Charlie. Why did you stop the train?"

"Why did you signal me to stop with the gong?" he replied.

"I didn't signal the stop!" the conductor shot back.

Charles said, "Well somebody did, and I'm not happy about it."

The conductor reminded Charles that Train 29 was coming up behind them. "Fire her up, Charlie. We've got to make up for lost time," the conductor said.

Charlie opened up the throttle to make extra time. But as he drove his train down the tracks, Charles Dawes started to worry about the Cohoke Bridge. As Charles got closer to the troublesome bridge, he cut back on the throttle and reduced speed. He scanned the track ahead by the light of the moon, but everything looked fine.

The train was approaching the Cohoke Bridge when Charles saw a light in the distance. It was the same swing lantern light that he had seen before. This time, however, it was swinging more frantically. Charles stretched his neck out of the cab and squinted his eyes in hopes of getting a closer look. At last, he saw it.

A long freight train was heading straight for him with its horns blowing and danger lights flashing. Charles started to bring his train to an emergency stop. The alarm gong began to sound. Obviously, the conductor had seen the oncoming train.

It's true that trains won't stop on a dime, but Charles was able to get his locomotive under control in record time. The train pulled up scarcely fifty yards from the Cohoke Bridge.

Charles and the conductor could see the fast freight barreling toward them.

"What's wrong with that fella? He's not even trying to stop!" hollered the conductor.

People leapt from the stopped train in anticipation of a major accident.

The oncoming train reached the bridge and raced onto it. As soon as it did, the metal bridge screamed and buckled, sending the freight train careening over the side. Its horn sounded as it rolled into the ground, sending dirt, smoke, and debris everywhere. Charles dove for cover. For what seemed like an eternity, the sounds of a crashing train filled Charlie Dawes' ears. Then, the sounds abruptly stopped.

When Charlie pulled himself together enough to survey the inevitable damage, he discovered that there wasn't any. No train or debris could be seen in the moonlight. Even the bridge stood firm. It wasn't long before one of the men behind him said the words that all of them were thinking: Ghost Train.

The crew heard the whistle of Train 29 approaching them from behind. Charles and the conductor made the decision to go ahead. But as Charles Dawes eased his beloved train over the Cohoke Bridge, he said a little prayer. "Dear Lord, please protect this train and all aboard it."

The rest of the night passed without incident. As Charles Dawes pulled into the yard, he couldn't help but hear his own words on the subject of trains. "Every time you hear a train whistle," he'd say, "you know that a new adventure is beginning for someone." He didn't know how right he was.

About the Author

Ian Alan is a psychic investigator and ghost hunter who has spent his life researching the enigmas and mysteries of the world. He is a teacher of ancient art and philosophy as well as a prolific free-lance writer. Ian Alan lives and writes in Birmingham, Alabama.